Harlequin, the world's No. 1 best-selling publisher of romance fiction, is proud of its tradition of bringing to women everywhere its beautiful and appealing love stories...

Harlequin Romances—warm and wholesome novels that take you to exciting faraway places and reveal the delights of true love.

Harlequin Presents—sophisticated and modern love stories that offer the thrill of exotic locales, and the passions and conflicts of love.

Superromance—longer, exciting, sensual and dramatic new novels, truly contemporary stories in keeping with today's life-styles.

What readers say about Harlequin romance fiction...

One Coin in the Fountain

by

ANITA CHARLES

Harlequin Books

TORONTO • LONDON • LOS ANGELES • AMSTERDAM
SYDNEY • HAMBURG • PARIS • STOCKHOLM • ATHENS • TOKYO

Original hardcover edition published in 1957
by Wright & Brown Limited

ISBN 0-373-01056-7

Harlequin edition published October 1966

Second printing December 1966
Third printing September 1972
Fourth printing February 1975
Fifth printing June 1975
Sixth printing June 1976
Seventh printing September 1978
Eighth printing June 1981

CHAPTER I

It was already dusk when the Paris plane touched down at London Airport. Rose Hereward stood shivering a little on the tarmac, feeling the keenness of the autumn wind after the pressurization and comfort of the interior of the aircraft, and she thought at first there was no one at all to meet her. And then she caught sight of Thatcher, her guardian's chauffeur, and a feeling of relief welled over her.

"Hello, Thatcher," she greeted him eagerly. "How nice to see you again!"

Thatcher's carefully controlled mask of an expression slipped a little as he returned her greeting.

"Nice to see you again, Miss Rose," he told her. He held open the rear door of his employer's sleek Bentley so that she could step in and make herself comfortable on the superbly sprung back seat, and escape the rawness of the wind; and then added more formally: "I trust you had a comfortable flight, miss?"

"Oh, yes," Rose relaxed with a faint sigh against the silver-grey upholstery. "Very comfortable, thank you, Thatcher." And then, with a little rush: "Sir Laurence is quite—quite well, I hope?"

"Very well, miss." Thatcher arranged a light rug over her knees, and then adjusted both windows so that only the right amount of cool night air would reach her. "Wedding plans going forward at a great pace, of course," shooting her a glance which puzzled her for a moment, until she realized that it contained a touch of apology. "Sir Laurence would have met you himself, only he

5

hardly has a moment to call his own these days. What with all the new arrivals and Farnhurst Manor already packed to the doors, as you might say, and a great deal of entertaining, and so forth. And naturally, Miss Willoughby——"

"Oh, of *course*, Thatcher," Rose reassured him at once, the colour rushing to her cheeks and burning them almost painfully. "Naturally, Miss Willoughby has prior claim these days, and I honestly didn't expect my guardian would find time to meet me."

She sounded as if she was horrified that anyone should imagine even for an instant that it had ever occurred to her that Sir Laurence, under the changed conditions, would find time to meet her. But as the big car slid forward and she rested her head against the back of the seat, the blush in her cheeks died slowly. For during the whole of the last half-hour while she was airborne she had kept two of her fingers tightly crossed, and had hoped against hope that the familiar figure would be there waiting for her at the airport.

It grew dark all at once, but by that time they were well away from London, following the course of the Great West Road. Rose wondered whether they were actually on their way to Dorset, and slid back the glass partition which separated her from the chauffeur and asked him what his instructions were.

"Are you taking me straight to Farnhurst, Thatcher?"

Thatched admitted that that was the plan.

"It was Sir Laurence's idea, Miss Rose. He thought you would prefer it to spending a night at the flat. And naturally he is in constant need of the car, and couldn't spare me, either, for any length of time."

"No, of course not," Rose agreed, like the expensively educated and well-disciplined young woman she was, and decided to ask no more questions.

But she was tired and a little hungry, for only tea had been served during the flight, and it looked as if dinner was something that had been overlooked in her case. Which was unlike Sir Laurence, for even when immersed in his own concerns, and preoccupied as she had often known him to be to such an extent that he seemed unaware of what was going on around him, the concerns of other people were never quite out of his mind. Especially when they were people with some sort of a claim on him.

She sighed as she watched the dark shapes of hedgerows sliding past the windows on either side of her in a slightly sinister fashion, and the occasional gleams in cottage windows as they sped through a village. The autumn-laden night air reached her through the narrow vent Thatcher had considered necessary; but although it cooled her cheeks, the sigh was repeated away down at the depths of her slender being. She wondered what Yvonne de Marsac, at whose parents' house in Paris she had spent last night, would think if she could see her now. She and Yvonne had passed the whole of last year together in Lausanne, at an exclusive establishment overlooking the lake, where their education had received a final polish, and until the abrupt news of Sir Laurence's engagement broke upon them Yvonne had been amusing herself with painting a picture of Rose's future.

"It will all work out quite romantically," she had declared, in spite of the fact that she was French, the daughter of an impecunious vicomte, with hard-headed notions about her own future. "You will marry the guardian, who has been waiting for you all these years——" But as Sir Laurence had been Rose's guardian for only five years she could never quite rise to this—"and it will in a sense be the marriage of convenience, because you will act as his housekeeper, and bring the feminine touch to his home, and be the light of his life during his declining years! You will make up to him for all his goodness and generosity to you, and it will not greatly matter that he is so many years older than you because——"

But here Rose had always interrupted hotly that her guardian was still in his early thirties, and that at that age a man was not old. Even by comparison with her own nineteen years he was not old! And, somehow, he had never struck her as old, but she did know he had been exceptionally generous to her. He had accepted the guardianship of her when he need have done nothing of the kind—when he must almost certainly have shrunk from the thought of having her thrust on him!—just because he had known and been very attached to her father, who had departed this world without leaving her a penny. All that she possessed today—every stitch of clothing belonging to her —was paid for out of the pockets of the man the world knew as a famous architect; a designer of so many lovely modern buildings that were the best of the age in which they sprang into being. Cathedrals, public buildings, blocks of palatial flats, even garden cities were linked with his name. He had received his knighthood two years before, while still on the sunny side of forty, and at the time Rose had felt so proud of him that her heart had actually seemed to swell inside her.

Now that she was nineteen she was still proud of him—proud to be known as his ward, proud to think that she shared a very small part of his life. And although she had listened to Yvonne's nonsense with an expression on her face which suggested she actually regarded it as arrant nonsense, Yvonne herself had not been deceived.

"You like him," she had declared, gleefully, more than once. "He is handsome—unless his photographs lie!—in a way that is more a distinguished kind of handsomeness than mere perfection of feature. Which means that his looks will not pall on you so easily!" She spoke as if she herself were twenty-nine, instead of not quite nineteen, and a woman of experience. "Once you see a little more of him it will be a simple matter to fall in love, for where there is no hardness of the head the heart is easily overcome. And your head is not in the least hard, my little one! Always you will ask for so little . . . So long as there is love!"

Her dark eyes glinted wickedly as Rose started to blush uncontrollably, although at the same time she insisted the other was talking absolute rubbish.

"No, it is not rubbish," Yvonne murmured softly, smoking a cigarette which was not allowed, but which had reached her in a parcel of confectionery dispatched by an obliging younger brother. "It is—how shall I say it in English?—a feeling I have, a touch of the *clairvoyance*. You will be Lady Melville, with a residence called Enderby—at which I will one day visit you, and stay for a very long while!—and as well as the all-important love," eyes glinting even more wickedly, "you will have, as you would put it, the 'extras'. The trimmings! You will have everything including the trimmings, and nothing could be more *convenable*. *N'est-ce pas?*"

But when the announcement of Sir Laurence's forth-coming marriage reached them even Yvonne felt slightly defrauded, as well as shocked. She had begun to believe in her own fairy story, and it was a distressing ending for a fairy story. Also neither of them knew anything at all about Miss Heather Willoughby, of Farnhurst Manor, in the county of Dorset, England.

But *The Times* plainly stated that Sir Laurence Melville, of Enderby, Glos., was to make her his wife.

And then began, in a whirlwind rush, all the plans for the wedding.

Sir Laurence wrote to his ward:

" . . . *I have talked to Heather about you, and she would very much like it if you would act as a bridesmaid at our wedding. Heather will be getting in touch with you herself about such things as measurements (no use expecting a mere man to obtain those correctly!) and any particular preference you have for colours. Also she is dying to meet you, and I am quite sure the two of you will get along excellenty together. I have, I'm afraid, rather laid it on with a trowel about my nice, obedient little ward! . . .*"

Rose felt the first actual twinge of uneasiness seize hold of her as she read those words again—*Nice, obedient little ward! . . .* What sort if picture would they conjure up in a woman's mind? For one thing, she, Rose, was not little—she was five feet five and a half inches in her stockinged feet, with all the grace and willowiness of the perfect model. Her hair flamed like russet leaves in the autumn, and her eyes—that she used to pretend to herself were hazel—were a clear, almost vivid, green! It was the colouring, as Yvonne had often told her, for a magazine cover, and there was nothing fake about it.

If Heather Willoughby was small, petite and pastel-tinted, how would she react to such a life-sized opposite to a *nice, obedient little ward?*

Rose thought uneasily that if it was no use expecting a mere man to obtain feminine measurements correctly, it was apparently just as little use to expect him to paint a portrait correctly—especially when he hadn't seen the subject of it for more than a year!

It was even possible he was in for a shock himself!

They did stop for dinner on the journey, and Rose was pleasurably surprised to learn that her guardian had not overlooked her comfort, and that he had issued particular instructions that the journey should be broken for a meal.

Thatcher was a little surprised when Rose put forward a shy plea for him to join her in the dining-room of the little inn where they eventually stopped, but having accepted the invitation he talked garrulously about the forthcoming wedding, and she learned many things she had not known previously. The honeymoon, for instance, was to be spent in Italy, and afterwards Sir Laurence was planning to take his bride to the Bahamas, where he would be working on plans for a new luxury hotel. It would be business combined with pleasure, and a kind of extended honeymoon until they returned to Enderby in the spring.

Enderby in the spring, thought Rose, with a kind of wistful nostalgia, and a sudden lump rising up in her throat which successfully took away all her appetite. Enderby was lovely at any season, but in spring, with the rolling hills and woods around it a tender haze of green, daffodils starring the long drive, and wallflowers blooming under the sheltered south terrace, it was a dream of a place. A genuine Tudor house Sir Laurence had bought in a state of dilapidation and worked over lovingly himself until it was all, and more, than anyone could desire.

Rose wished she was going straight to Enderby now, instead of a strange house packed with guests, not one of whom she knew.

When they arrived, although another half-hour would usher in midnight, lights streamed from every window and down the rhododendron-lined drive. There were cars still lining the drive, too, which seemed to indicate that the evening had

11

been marked by either a formal dinner-party or an informal dance. From the fact that music was also finding its way out into the night, Rose deduced the latter.

She was admitted by an extremely correct-looking manservant, and a maid took her cases from Thatcher. Then the same maid conducted her upstairs to her room, which struck her as extremely luxurious after the spartan-like austerity of the room she had shared with Yvonne in Lausanne.

"Miss Willoughby said you would probably want supper," the maid said, once the cases were deposited on an oak rest at the foot of the bed. Rose had barely time to take in that the carpet was mushroom-pink, the satin bedspread and quilted bed-head mushroom-pink also, before she was expected to retrace her steps downstairs again, and admitted to a dining-room full of sombre magnificence where she discovered she was to be the only occupant.

A corner of the table was laid with lace table-mats, some glittering glass and silverware, and a bowl of fruit, and hot soup was brought to her. It was followed by a portion of cold chicken which, however, she declined, and asked instead if she could have some coffee. When the coffee arrived she was left in peace and isolation to drink it slowly, and while she did so those softened strains of music reached her, as well as the gay murmur of distant voices.

It was just as if around her the house was alive and vibrating eagerly, but the room in which she sat was a quiet pool of shadow, pierced by the flickering flames of tall, branching, Georgian candlesticks on the table in front of her. The table was massive old oak, and in its polished surface the candlelight was reflected like stars peering at their reflection in a still sheet of water. The enormous silver bowl of piled up peaches and grapes

12

looked unreal and nebulous floating in the midst of such a sea.

Rose decided that it was because she was tired, but she had a sensation of being cut off and forgotten, marooned in an isolation where no one would find her—where no one wished to find her! Her arrival had created as much impression as a pebble flung into the middle of the Atlantic would do, and so far as she was aware no one, apart from two members of the domestic staff, was even aware that she had arrived.

She was wondering how she would ever find her way back to her room in this rambling house when voices immediately outside the stout oak door caused her to sit upright and tense herself. One of the voices was bubbling with a honeyed kind of merriment, although it also seemed to be expostulating at the same time, and the other was deep and masculine. As the door opened the masculine voice that caused Rose's breath to remain suddenly stilled in her throat was saying:

"It's not too late to meet her, Heather! And, after all, I must say something to the child!"

Rose stood up, feeling all in a moment more painfully self-conscious than she had ever felt in her life before. She turned to face the door, and behind her the candles flamed, and her glorious Titian hair seemed to be irradiated by them. She was wearing a simple but well-cut lime-green suit, and the exquisite slenderness of her figure was emphasized by it. She looked pale—a kind of magnolia pallor—and her eyes were enormous under their sweeping lashes.

She didn't know it, but she looked rare—rare and exotic, and utterly unlike a schoolgirl with no knowledge at all of the world. Already, and in spite of hours of travel, she had a shy poise, and a gentle elegance. No one could possibly dismiss her as a nice, obedient little ward—and nothing more!

13

Heather Willoughby, who looked like a fairy on the Christmas tree with her floating cloud of golden hair, her china blue eyes, and her white net dress—yards and yards of net billowing round her like a cloud—was conscious of a distinct sensation of shock. And it was not a pleasant shock.

"But you *can't* be Rose!" she exclaimed. "Not the little Rose who is to be my youngest bridesmaid?"

Rose felt as if her tongue became animated all at once.

"But you received my measurements," she said gently. "They must have prepared you for the fact that I'm not really little."

"Little?" The fly-away eyebrows arched. "You're a good many inches taller than I am! A good six inches, I should say! And I'll admit I merely handed your measurements over to the dressmaker and told her to get on with your dress."

She laughed suddenly, looking up sideways at her fiancé.

"Well, haven't you anything to say to your *little* ward, Lance?"

Laurence Melville was standing with his hands in the pockets of his admirably-tailored dinner-jacket, looking at Rose. He was looking at her with something in his eyes that would have caused her to feel amused under other circumstances, for in addition to surprise there was a quizzical gleam, a faintly disbelieving gleam, in the cool grey glance she remembered. The past year had added a touch of frost to the dark-brown hair at his temples, but otherwise he was exactly as she remembered him — as she had thought of him so often — tall, and hard, and spare, with a masculine grace that was unusual.

"As a matter of fact, Rose," he admitted, "you have shot up rather alarmingly since I saw you last! Have you been sampling a bottle labelled 'drink me'?"

Rose felt herself flushing almost guiltily as his eyes dwelt on her. The quizzical gleam disconcerted her.

"I suppose I've just—just grown up," she answered, and felt as if the animation had left her tongue, and she was fumbling for words.

He had never kissed her in the whole course of their acquaintance, but he walked up to her now and put his hands on her shoulders. He looked down at her smilingly.

"And done it very nicely, Rose," he said softly. "Very, very nicely!"

She felt herself blushing more painfully than ever.

Heather interrupted, her voice as brittle as a Japanese windmill.

"Well, you mustn't keep the child out of her bed any longer, Lance! You forget that she flew over from Paris this afternoon and has had a long drive since then." She turned a carefully conjured-up smile on Rose. "You and I have simply *got* to get to know one another, my dear," she said, "and tomorrow we'll have a lovely long talk, and you can try on your bridesmaid's dress, and we'll see how you look in it. With your hair you should look quite ravishing, because it's an utterly enchanting pale primrose-stalk green. And you'll meet all the other bridesmaids, of course —there's three of them staying in the house."

Then she turned and slipped her hand possessively inside Lance's arm, and almost tugged him away in the direction of the door.

"Come along, darling—leave Rose to finish her coffee, and you, too, can have a talk with her in the morning. But it's late now!"

"Too late for Rose to be drinking coffee," he said, a little critically, his gaze still fixed on the slight figure of his ward. "Would you like some hot milk sent up to you, Rose?" thinking how

15

utterly weary she looked, and how young, in spite of her graceful height, and soft air of sophistication.

"No, thank you." She shook her head. "No, thank you very much."

"Sure?" His eyes smiled at her again. "You may be eighteen, but it's still an excellent sedative after a long journey."

"I'm not eighteen," she heard herself saying awkwardly. "I had my nineteenth birthday last week."

"Oh!" For an instant his eyebrows ascended and he looked quite shocked. "And I forgot it!"

"It didn't matter." She still sounded awkward, but she smiled at him tremulously. "Of course I understood."

Heather looked up at him, a bright sparkle in her eyes.

"She understood that you had other preoccupations, darling—which, of course, you had! And now do let us return to our guests!"

CHAPTER II

THE following day Rose was introduced to so many people that her head was dizzy long before lunch-time. There were the three young women who were to share with her the experience—in Rose's case the only experience in her nineteen years so far—of escorting a bride to the altar of the village church; and there were a couple of gay young men cast for the "rôles" of ushers. There was also another very handsome young man, by the name of Peter Hurst, who looked, Rose thought, a trifle despondent sometimes—particularly when Heather was behaving as if the sole reason for her existence was the man she was to marry. Sometimes, however, she took a kind of kittenish delight in tantalizing Sir Laurence a little, pleading all sorts of whirlwind engagements, such as hairdressing appointments, appointments with dressmakers, jewellers — her mother was having a large amount of old-fashioned family jewellery reset for her—shoemakers (the kind that specialized in hand-sewn footwear only), etc., that would keep them apart for a time. But on other occasions she was completely adoring, the lovely clinging vine living only for her wedding day, and it was on these occasions Rose noticed that Peter Hurst looked rather more than *distrait*.

Then there was the bride-elect's godmother, a Mrs. Wilson-Plunkett, also staying in the house. Rose found herself curiously drawn to Mrs. Wilson-Plunkett, one reason being that she enjoyed her somewhat caustic sense of humour, and she was intrigued by her definitely eccentric manner of dressing. She wore bunches of dyed curls bobbing on her forehead—and her age was a thing

17

which could only be guessed at—evening dresses of satin and velvet that had an Edwardian flavour, and was always smothered in jewellery. No matter the hour at which she appeared outside her room she invariably dripped diamonds, and her pearls were magnificent.

Heather was always noticeably anxious that her godmother should receive every attention, and never under any circumstances be neglected; and Rose decided that this was because Mrs. Wilson-Plunkett was obviously a very rich widow. And then she instantly took herself to task for thinking such a mercenary thought about her guardian's future wife. For, in spite of the fact that she herself had been more or less consistently ignored by the bride-to-be since the night of her arrival, and they had not so far had that "lovely long talk" Heather had expressed herself as looking forward to, she had such an unshakable belief in the natural shrewdness and common-sense of Sir Laurence that she was sure he would not have picked a woman to share his whole future life who was not, under the somewhat dazzling façade she presented to the world, essentially *nice*—in the way Rose youthfully understood niceness.

And although Heather struck her as almost too radiantly lovely at times—a slightly brittle loveliness, like the note that occasionally invaded her high-pitched laughter—and as the only child of elderly, doting parents who were straining every nerve and all their resources to give her a memorable wedding, she was undoubtedly both spoiled and pampered, she could, when she chose, exert a good deal of charm. Appeal was probably a better word—an extremely feminine appeal that got under the skins of the masculine element in the house, and made them anxious to obey her lightest behest.

Rose was often amazed to see Lance looking on with complacency in the evenings whilst she queened it in the midst of a large circle of obvious admirers. Wearing something new and expensive that bore the hall-mark of a top-ranking *couturier*, enclosed in an aura of delicate Paris perfume, she distributed her favours with such gay impartiality that anyone old-fashioned amongst the guests, considering that she was planning to be married so soon, might have looked a little askance. But the smile on Lance's lips was invariably indulgent, the look in his eyes completely adoring. It was plain to everyone that he was a man very, very much in love, and Rose found that something difficult to understand.

She found it difficult to understand because the Laurence Melville she had thought she knew was a man she had frequently seen looking extremely cynical, had frequently heard expressing cynical, hard-headed opinions. There had been nothing about him to suggest that underneath his hard-bitten exterior he was quite dangerously vulnerable—to such an extent that a golden-headed will-o'-the-wisp like Heather Willoughby could suddenly turn him into a more or less abject slave. If, Rose thought, she had been a woman of a slightly different type — one whose mentality would enable her to share his interests later on, who would make his interests her interests, and demand less in the way of admiration. . . .

But she obviously throve on admiration, and she certainly justified it. Also she was twenty-six, and at that age no doubt most women had learned something about the art of captivating male hearts. About the value of sheer glamour.

Rose felt certain that if Yvonne de Marsac had been amongst the guests at Farnhurst Manor she would have held forth on the subject of glamour. She would probably have declared it was the one thing no true woman could afford to be without, and every wise woman sought to cultivate.

In which case Rose was afraid she was singularly lacking in the commodity, for although she

19

sometimes saw admiration in masculine eyes, she was not sought after like the other young women who helped to swell the guests.

But everyone was roped in for the purpose of performing some useful function, and Rose spent the better part of those days before the wedding helping to unpack wedding presents as they arrived, and displaying them to advantage in the panelled library of the manor. And when the discovery was made that she could type she was kept busy sending off acknowledgments, and dealing with other items of relative correspondence that might otherwise have been overlooked. Mrs. Wilson-Plunkett, who seemed to have taken quite a fancy to her, declared she was too willing, and advantage was being taken of her willingness, but Rose didn't really mind.

She preferred spending whole days quietly in the library at a typewriter to joining the other young people in their constant and somewhat hectic search for entertainment. They were such sophisticated young people, and they made her feel young and stupid, and over-conscious of the fact that she had only just left her schooldays behind.

Sometimes she was even sent on messages to the village when every telephone line was engaged, and it was impossible to get through to such people as Miss Mackintosh, who was generously lending valuable china and glass for the reception after the wedding, or Colonel Carpenter, at The White House, who had promised hothouse blooms, including orchids, to form part of the decoration in the church. Or little Mrs. Annie Moss, who was a skilled embroidress, and working on part of Heather's more intimate trousseau.

It was when she was on her way to Mrs. Moss on the third afternoon after Thatcher had safely delivered her at Farnhurst that Rose caught a glimpse of her guardian's car streaking through

20

the village ahead of her. It was a lovely village, with a square-towered Norman church, a well-tended green, and even a pond with ducks quacking on it, and Sir Laurence's big car looked a little incongruous coming to rest outside the tiny post office.

Rose, who had been enjoying the soft warmth of the early October afternoon—almost as good as a return to summer, she thought, with the crisp leaves underfoot, a genial sun in her face, and the hedgerows burgeoning afresh with a blaze of scarlet berries—and was not in any particular hurry, when she realized that her guardian was sitting waiting for her. He was alone in the car, and she could see his dark, handsome profile turned sideways to watch the narrow sidewalk, and with her heart beating more quickly she increased her pace.

"Get in, Rose," he said, gently, as he held open the door for her. "I don't seem to have seen anything at all of you since you arrived."

"Oh, but I'm on my way to Mrs. Moss," she explained. I don't think I ought to waste any time."

"And who," he asked, smiling, "is Mrs. Moss?"

"She's a wonderful embroidress, and lives in the village—she's working on part of Miss Willoughby's trousseau."

"Don't you think you could bring yourself to say Heather?" he inquired, his smile twisting a little oddly.

"Oh, er—y-yes, of course."

"Good!" he exclaimed, softly. "You'll be seeing quite a lot of one another in future, you know."

He agreed to drop her outside Mrs. Moss's cottage, but urged her not to be long.

"And when you've finished discussing these important details on behalf of Heather we'll go for a little drive," he said. "There are one or two

21

things I must talk to you about, and this seems a splendid opportunity."

Rose couldn't imagine what it was he wanted to talk to her about particularly, but she was glad that there was no excuse for lingering inside Annie Moss's cluttered living-room, for the exquisite hand-tucked nylon nightdresses were ready, and the three sets of underwear were all-but ready. She was able to carry away with her the nightdresses and place them, protected by layers of tissue-paper and a stout cardboard box, almost reverently on the back seat of the car, and then Lance once again held open the door for her. She slipped into the seat beside the driving-seat and realized that this was the first time she had been really close to him for more than a year—apart from those few minutes when he had welcomed her on the night of her arrival.

"Now," he said, "I think we'll go into Rington and have some tea, shall we? Would you like that?"

"Of course," she answered, "if you're quite sure you—I mean," haltingly, "if you don't think that Heather——?"

"Heather is very much preoccupied this afternoon," he told her. "And in any case I am occasionally allowed to devote a little time to my ward," smiling again in the fashion she thought a trifle odd.

"Oh, of course," she agreed, feeling herself flushing. "I wasn't suggesting that you have to ask her permission."

"I should hope not!" he exclaimed, and she thought all at once his tone sounded quite grim, as well as emphatic.

When they reached Rington he drove her at once to the George, an ancient and delightful half-timbered hostelry standing flush with the main street, where they served afternoon teas in an atmosphere of log fires and peaceful old oak.

Although it happened to be a market-day, and later the place would be crowded, at that early hour of the afternoon it was still comparatively empty, and they were provided with a table quite close to the fire. Sir Laurence ordered tea and toast and lots of cakes—"with cream," he added, looking at Rose in a twinkling fashion as if he still secretly regarded her as very young indeed —and then remembered that she was actually a young woman and offered her a cigarette while they waited.

"Now, tell me," he said, "what you're going to do with yourself while Heather and I are away."

Rose look quite confounded.

"I don't think I've actually thought about it," she confessed.

"I'm afraid you will have to think of it," he warned her, gently. "You've finished with Lausanne, and in fact you're now a very finished product indeed"—flashing her his most charming smile—"but there still remains the problem of what precisely is to become of you while your legal guardians are away."

The waiter carried a loaded tray to their table, and Rose waited while he set forth the flowery pieces of china, and then placed a hot chafing-dish at her elbow. She poised the sugar-tongs above her guardian's cup, asked the usual question, and passed him his tea before she replied at last in a somewhat subdued tone.

"I think the best thing I can do is to get a job as quickly as possible, don't you? I'm quite a competent shorthand-typist—we learned that sort of thing at Gerhardt—and I've also quite a flair for languages. I can go and stay in Paris with Yvonne until I actually land myself a job, and as she's job-hunting, too, we can go in for it together."

But her guardian, who had been staring thoughtfully at the tip of his cigarette and had declined any of the tempting edibles, looked up at her with a faint frown between his brows.

"I don't know that I approve of that idea at all."

"Why not?" she asked.

The frown grew more noticeable as he looked across the table at her—at her lovely flame of red hair surrounding the perfect heart-shaped face, her extraordinarily lustrous and unusual eyes, her lovely sensitive mouth, and slender column of a throat. She was wearing a heather-mixture tweed suit today, with a plain little white blouse below it, and as the collar of the white blouse was round and puritan it somehow lent her a puritan look, too. An unsullied look.

"For one thing, I'm not at all sure that I approve of your friend Yvonne——" He crushed out his cigarette in the ash-tray and lighted another. "She's rather a light-hearted young woman, if I remember rightly, most unmistakably French, and I couldn't view the prospect of your careering round Paris under her auspices with anything like equanimity. And I don't think the present time is a good time to discuss your taking on any sort of a job. Later on we will discuss it—but not now!"

"And in the meantime?" she asked quietly.

"You could stay on at the Manor. The Willoughbys would be delighted to have you, and would treat you like a daughter."

But Rose shook her head.

"I'm afraid I couldn't agree to that. Whatever happens, I mean to be independent."

Sir Laurence smiled.

"Not of me, too?"

"Yes," she surprised him by answering quite definitely, "of you, too!" As his dark eyebrows ascended she rushed on: "My father asked you to look after me, I know, but it wasn't—it never has been!—a legal arrangement. You have been most kind—more than kind!—particularly as you have had to spend your own money on me for years, but that is one reason why I have firmly made up my mind that I am going to free you of the responsibility of looking after me—of concerning yourself about my future! I'm old enough and capable enough now to concern myself about my own future."

"Indeed?" His voice was suddenly soft and rather drawling. "And for how long have you been thinking along these lines?"

She made a small, shrugging movement with her slim shoulders.

"Oh, for a long time!"

"Ever since I decided to get married?" dryly.

"Perhaps."

"Or ever since you met Heather?"

"Please," she begged, "I don't want to seem ungrateful, but you must believe me when I say that I am completely serious. Now that you are marrying Miss Will—Heather, I couldn't possibly go on thinking of you as a guardian! It would be different if—if I *had* to think of you as a guardian—but you know as well as I do that I don't! And in fairness to Miss—to Heather—"

"Whom you don't like!"

"It isn't that at all! She's a young woman getting married for the first time, and how could she possibly look with any sort of pleasure on the idea of a ready-made family? And, in any case, I am *not* your family, I am really nothing to do with you, and I want to launch out on my own..."

She hadn't meant to say all this when she started, but somehow the words had poured from her, and she felt tremendously relieved when she had given them vent. For to have gone on with the idea of one day living with him and Heather—once Heather was his wife!—had become such a revolting idea that she knew she couldn't bear it. Heather would very quickly let him see that *she* couldn't bear it—she would pick on the absence of any legal ties—and life would be impossible for Rose.

25

"You are talking the utmost nonsense," Sir Laurence declared, looking at her as if she had succeeded in disturbing and dismaying him, "and all that I can think of is that this endless fuss about the wedding has upset you in some curious way. But I promised your father that I would look after you, and I mean to go on doing so— until someone else has the right, at any rate!— and since you've reminded me that you're not legally my ward I'll take the necessary steps at once to ensure that you are. You needn't think that just because you're nineteen you're beyond all need of future guidance——"

"I don't, oh, I don't!" she assured him, looking at him with penitence and pleading — and she hoped so much he realized how grateful she was for all that he had already done for her—and his eyes softened before the distress in her face.

"Be a good girl, Rose," he coaxed, "and don't rush your fences! Stay at the Manor at least until I get back from my honeymoon."

"But that will be — that will be a long time," she faltered.

"A month," he replied, "a month in Italy. And after that we're going to the Bahamas. But there's no reason at all why you shouldn't come with us to the Bahamas."

Rose felt suddenly acutely wistful instead of rebellious. No reason? She wondered what Heather would have to say to that.

"Give me your promise that you'll stay at the Manor with the Willoughbys for at least a month," he insisted.

Rose realized that just then it would be unfair to withhold that promise from him. She couldn't let him go away on his honeymoon with a mind disturbed by any back-thoughts about her.

"Very well," she said, "I'll promise you that. . ."

CHAPTER III

WHEN they arrived back at Farnhurst, Heather was waiting for them in the hall.

One look at her face told Rose that she was angry. In fact, she appeared to be seething with resentment and indignation.

"I couldn't *think* what had happened to you, Lance!" she declared. She shot a stormily furious look at Rose. "The Carters called this afternoon directly I got back from my fitting, and they brought their wedding present with them. It's a simply lovely pair of antique silver salvers, and I felt so absolutely stupid when I couldn't even tell them where you were, although you were supposed to be somewhere around. Naturally, it never *occurred* to me that you had taken your ward for a drive!"

"Why naturally?" Lance inquired in a peculiarly quiet voice. "Is it a crime to take my ward for a drive?"

Heather turned away from him. Her whole attitude told him that her annoyance was not in the least likely to simmer down quickly, and the way she tossed her golden head drove home the extent of that annoyance. While Rose placed the cardboard box containing the nylon nightdresses on the hall table, the daughter of the house swept through into the empty dining-room; but her fiancé did not follow her. He went straight upstairs to his room, and Rose, following at a discreet distance behind him, thought miserably that she had been the cause of what might well be his first quarrel with Heather.

That night it seemed to her that they had still not made it up, for Heather was looking sulky and remote, and Lance had a grave detached look in his face. Rose had seen that look before, when she had wanted to approach him for some purpose and it had seemed to her that he had erected a wall between himself and the world of mundane things. It had been a wall she had always hestitated to attempt to scale—but Heather, she felt sure, had more courage. In addition to which Heather must know him immeasurably better than she, Rose, could ever hope to do.

At dinner, although there was a lot of merriment amongst the guests, it scarcely spread to the couple who were so soon to take one another for better or worse. They noticeably avoided saying anything very pointed to one another, and gradually their frozen attitudes affected the demeanour of the guests. Eyebrows were raised, looks exchanged—the bride's mother looked faintly perturbed. And Rose felt more and more weighted down by a burden of guilt.

But after dinner, when the carpet in the drawing-room was rolled back for dancing, the engaged couple were the first to take the floor, and an almost audible sigh of relief went through the long, low room. For, even if Heather's smile was not as unclouded as usual as she directed it up into her fiancé's face, at least she was smiling at him, and if there had been any danger of the wedding not taking place after all, that danger seemed now to have receded.

Rose danced one or two dances with young men who asked her—although none of them made any attempt to detain her for long; perhaps because her conversation was not of a sufficiently light-hearted and sparkling order—and at ten o'clock she decided to go upstairs to bed. But on her way she passed the library door, and an impulse caused her to enter it to collect a book from the shelves. No sooner, however, had she turned the handle and softly pushed open the door than the most extraordinary conviction rushed over her that she would have been wiser to have foregone reading matter for that night.

The room was in darkness, but as soon as her hand pressed the switch the two figures standing close together near the window became flood-lighted, as it were, by mellow golden gleams. They were two figures standing very quietly in one another's arms, and at the moment the light went on the girl's lips were upturned in complete and blissful surrender to the man, and the man was easily recognizable as Peter Hurst.

Rose stood for a moment as if transfixed, and then she turned back hastily to the door. But before she could beat a retreat and recover to a certain extent her composure Heather Willoughby, without uttering a sound to the man, had detached herself swiftly from his arms and crossed the room and caught Rose firmly by the shoulders.

"No, don't run away, Rose!" the bride-to-be said softly. "There's something I want to show you, if you'll come upstairs to my room! My going-away outfit arrived this morning, and I haven't yet had a chance to try it on. Come with me, and you shall tell me just how nice I look in it, or whether the bill was too steep!"

Her voice had the sweetness of honey and the cooing of pigeons in it, but her eyes were hard and bright and full of a sinister warning. The warning was so unmistakable that Rose found it impossible to think up an excuse that would still have enabled her to escape, or even to register disapproval of what she had just witnessed. She was secretly so shocked by what she had seen that she even wondered in a kind of numb, confused way whether she had imagined it, especially as Heather's scarlet lips were parted over her milky little even teeth in a smile of peculiar brilliance.

"Come along, Rose," she repeated, and urged her with gentle force from the room.

29

But, upstairs in her own room—a room with an almost pure white carpet, pale primrose walls and ceiling, and a bed with a kind of canopy of draped white velvet above it—she suddenly shed the mask of friendliness and revealed claws far sharper than even Rose had suspected existed inside her lacquered finger-nails.

"So you add prying to your other accomplishments, do you?" she said, turning on Rose with unleashed fury. "All the things you learned at that expensive finishing-school of yours in Lausanne, for which Lance paid your fees! Well, let me warn you, my dear, that if you so much as breathe a word of what you saw tonight to any-one—*anyone*, inside or outside this house!—I'll open Lance's eyes to one or two things about you! In particular one thing! . . . I'll let him know that far from being a tractable little ward you've already fallen in love with him! It's so obvious to me, and has been from the night you arrived, that he ought to be aware of it himself, but he's simple in some ways! Those moon-struck eyes of yours don't convey a thing to him, but I realized immediately that one day you might become a nuisance, and I'll see that Lance is put on his guard—*if you're so indiscreet as to give me away!*"

Rose shrank back as if the other had actually struck her, and the venom in Heather's voice was enough to make anyone unprepared for it recoil. But, at the same time, Rose felt sick and appalled —appalled because her guardian was to marry this woman, and because she herself had been accused of something she could not deny.

"And now you can go," Heather said, icily, indicating the door. "But don't forget I meant every word I said just now! *Every* word! So if you think you've got me in the palm of your hand—think again!"

CHAPTER IV

THE day of the wedding drew nearer, and confusion reigned at Farnhurst Manor. There was a constant stream of tradesmen's vans driving up to the impressive front door, and express delivery boys, telegraph boys—because the telephone lines were always choked, and the village postmistress gave up trying to transmit telegrams over them —added to the congestion in the winding drive. The man responsible for the catering arrangements came and went, and it was discovered that the seating arrangements for the wedding breakfast were inadequate, and the whole plan had to be revised, and Colonel Carpenter was persuaded to supply Hepplewhite chairs as well as the greater part of the floral decorations.

The day before the wedding the wedding-dress and the bridesmaids' dresses arrived from London in a special van. All four bridesmaids went into ecstasies over the lovely creations of palest green organza they were to wear, and although Rose's ecstasies were a little more subdued than the others, it was not because her own particular dress failed to arouse as much admiration. She was feminine enough to realize that a more suitable colour could not have been chosen for herself, and as there were long gloves of lavender suede to go with the dresses, lavender straw bonnets, and bouquets of half-opened yellow rosebuds to be carried on the day, the colour-scheme was well-nigh perfect.

The wedding dress, and the beauties of it, were to be kept a secret until the bride appeared in the aisle of the ancient village church on the arm of her father, and everyone had a chance to admire.

31

But one look at Heather's face when she re-appeared downstairs after remaining closeted with her mother upstairs in her bedroom for some little while, with the dress almost certainly spread out on the bed to gaze at, convinced Rose that the bride was entirely satisfied. She looked like a cat that had greedily lapped up all the cream, and was temporarily altogether content. It was only as the hours between her and her wedding started to diminish until anyone very dull at arithmetic would count them easily that her temper started to become noticeably rather short, and sometimes there was a slightly strained expression on her fair-skinned face.

Rose she almost entirely ignored, but whether her guardian noticed it Rose was unable to tell. She was in too unhappy a state of mind in those days to care very much about anything, and the only thing that constantly troubled her was the remembrance of that night in the library. She had made up her mind that whatever she saw that night it had really nothing to do with herself, and that under no circumstances could she have offered anything in the nature of a warning to Sir Laurence. For one thing, he would probably not have believed her—very few men are willing to believe ill of the woman they were going to marry almost on the very eve of the wedding—and for another, if Heather had carried out her threat and informed him that his ward (whom he still looked upon as an undeveloped child!) had formed a far warmer attachment for him than a ward normally feels for a guardian, it would look very much as if her story of what took place in the library was coloured largely by jealousy, and for that reason alone could be discounted.

No; Rose decided that if disillusionment was to come to Laurence Melville it would have to come *after* his marriage, and not before. She felt heavier at heart than she had ever felt in her life before as she made this decision, and if exposure of her own feelings for him could have guaranteed him nothing but happiness in the future she would willingly have submitted to Heather making a kind of mock of her. For there are some things, in certain causes, one can endure—and Rose would have endured a great deal for Sir Lance.

Mrs. Wilson-Plunkett, who spent her days observing people and their various reactions, did not fail to observe that on Rose's face sometimes, when she was looking at her guardian and the woman he was to marry, there was a very unchildlike look of doubt, and even a vague anxiety.

"You're not very happy about this match, are you?" she said to the girl once. "Well, I wouldn't worry," as Rose looked around at her in instant concern, because apparently she kept so little guard over what she was thinking and feeling. "Modern marriages are more like trial engagements, I often think, and so often they don't stand up to even the period of trial. It was different when I was young. Then a young woman didn't enter into a contract which should, of course, be binding with the back-thought in her head that, if everything didn't turn out as she hoped it would, she could go home to mother, or simply cut loose and get herself a job, and later on another husband! Husbands in those days were permanent institutions, like the home, and the background of family life."

Rose noted the cynical expression of her face and sought to defend her generation.

"I shouldn't think there are very many young women who actually marry with the thought that their marriage could be anything other than permanent."

"No?" a strongly cynical note in the rather harsh voice. "Well, I don't imagine you would, because with that hair of yours there will never be any half measures where you're concerned,

33

and you're the type I should think, to remain loyal under any circumstances. But my god-daughter and your guardian are oil and water—they'll never mix! He's old enough to know it, but there's nothing quite so besotted as a man in love, and he'll take his awakening very hardly when it comes! I'll give them a couple of years at the outside!"

"Oh, no!" Rose exclaimed.

"Oh, yes, child!" The shrewd old eyes beneath the bobbing false curls seemed to mock her gently. "And, in your heart of hearts, don't you think that yourself? Haven't you got some doubts? You know that Sir Laurence is a serious man at heart —a very serious man—and Heather lives simply for the gratification of all her creature instincts. For her this is a good match — an excellent match—and her parents know it as well. She's extravagant, and only a well-to-do man could give her all she needs. Sir Laurence is rather more than well-to-do."

"But, there must be—there must be something more than that . . ." Rose said, hoping ardently for her guardian's sake that what she was saying was no more than truth.

"Must there?" They were walking in the sunken rose garden, where the paths were littered with fallen petals, and the air was heavy with perfume in spite of the lateness of the season, and the fact that only a few blooms were still at their best, and Mrs. Wilson-Plunkett was leaning heavily on a slender ebony cane that tap-tapped sharply on the flags. "Well, in a couple of years time we'll all know just what there is—or, rather, was! But when a man with a good deal of intelligence starts to remember his old interests, and those interests are not shared by the woman with whom he has imagined himself spending the rest of his life, well—that's the time when almost anything might happen!"

Rose walked on quietly ahead of her, and when they came to a white-painted garden seat Mrs. Wilson-Plunkett insisted on sitting down.

"I'm not as young as I was, and I get tired easily," she said. As usual, she was sparkling with ornamentation, and her coquettish but old-fashioned hat was trimmed with expensive mink that matched the cape about her bony shoulders. Sometimes Rose found herself wondering exactly how old she was, and decided that in order to hazard a guess one would have to see her without the make-up she applied liberally to all the exposed portions of her face and neck. "And now let's forget about the 'happy pair' for the time being," she continued surprisingly, "and talk about you."

"Me?" Rose looked round at her in astonishment.

"Yes, my dear, you!" Mrs. Wilson-Plunkett actually beamed at her kindly. "What are you going to do with yourself once Sir Laurence goes off and leaves you? You're his ward, aren't you? What arangements has he made for your future?"

Rose explained that her guardian desired her to stay on for a time at the Willoughbys, and the old lady made a clucking noise of disagreement and displeasure.

"All wrong! Stuck away here in the heart of the country when you've only just finished with being a school-girl! That won't do at all! You must come and stay with me. I've a flat in town where I spend a few months of every year, and the remaining months I travel. You must join me on my travels! No use talking to your guardian—he isn't capable of listening to anything that doesn't concern his beloved at the moment, so there's no use wasting time on him. We'll just write to him and tell what I'm doing with you once I've actually started to do it."

"Oh, but—" Rose exclaimed.

"No buts! You'd *like* to come away with me, wouldn't you?"

Rose felt a temporary uplifting of her heart, a sudden resurgence of her spirit. Above everything else she wished to become completely independent of her guardian and his bride, and if Mrs. Wilson-Plunkett meant that she would employ her. . . .

"You—you do mean that, don't you?" she stammered. "That you want a — a companion, or a secretary, or something——?"

"You can put it like that if you like," the old lady answered with a smile. "I'll pay you a salary—I'm a very rich woman, I don't mind telling you, and I'll pay you a very generous salary—and in return you can play chess with me in the evenings, read to me and answer a few of my letters. And we'll travel about the world together, and I'll pay all your expenses. I like you, my dear — your hair is just the colour mine used to be, the colour of autumn leaves. I think you're the loveliest young woman I've ever seen, and with a little pride taken in you, a little money spent on you . . ." She nodded her head as if she was suddenly immensely pleased with her own idea, and could see that idea expanding most satisfactorily. "Yes; leave it to me, child, and we'll get away from here as soon as this wedding's over. Do you know Venice? Have you seen Rome? . . . No? . . . Well, wait until you've seen the Colosseum by moonlight! . . . Wait until you've seen the spires of Florence! . . . I love Italy. It will be a pleasure for me to take you there. . . ."

And she went on and on, bemusing Rose with her talk of fascinating corners of the world, and making it impossible for her to interrupt because by degrees she didn't want to interrupt. And although she felt certain her guardian would have to be consulted—that the least she could do after all his kindness to her was to consult him—just then she had to be content with waiting to drive

36

that point home to Mrs. Wilson-Plunkett at a later stage.

But the last few hours before the wedding was due to take place hardly presented an opportunity to discuss anything at all with her guardian, and she gathered he took it for granted that she would be remaining with the Willoughbys. The afternoon before the wedding they had a rehearsal in the village church, and some idea of the beauty of the ceremony was conveyed to all of them— and most keenly to Rose—because already the setting was massed with flowers, and the organist was practising in the organ loft. Rose remembered that afternoon for the rest of her life, and even while she watched the effect of the sunlight through the stained-glass window behind the altar falling across the chancel steps, where the two leading figures stood, she had the feeling that for her it was an afternoon with an acute personal significance. But she failed to understand what exactly the significance was.

After the rehearsal was over Sir Laurence drove himself into Rington, where he proposed to spend his last night as a bachelor, and to entertain a few friends of his own sex. It was not exactly a stag-party, but it was somethng in the same nature, and left Heather free to go to bed early and prepare herself for the great day ahead of her.

When that day dawned everyone within the house was glad that it showed every promise of being a spectacularly beautiful autumn day. And by noon that promise was assured. There was clear sky and gently falling golden sunshine, just enough breeze to lift the ends of the bride's veil and catch playfully at the wide skirts of her bridesmaids, and just enough sparkling freshness in the air to make the sound of the bells carry far and wide. When Rose first heard them they were pealing out across the woods and meadows, and she herself was in the back of a big and gleaming car decorated with white ribbons with the other three bridesmaids and on her way to the church.

At the lych-gate there was the usual little crowd of villagers to receive them, the usual admiring looks were shot at her and her companions, and then a beautifully turned-out usher assisted them from the car. They stood grouped in the porch while they waited for the bride, and behind them in the church the organ played softly, and Rose knew that rows and rows of relatives and friends of both the prospective bride and bridegroom were waiting with bated breath and a good deal of nervous tension for the moment when the little procession that was to form the highlight of their day would enter and sweep down the aisle.

Rose herself felt ridiculously nervous and strung up—far more nervous, she was sure, than Heather herself was feeling, although with far more cause. She could picture her and her father left behind alone at the Manor—if they were not already on their way in the car—and Heather's deliberate last-minute concern with her appearance. Completely satisfied with the way she looked, she would know no shyness, and it was her father who would be the most fussed. Rose had always felt inclined to pity him a little, for he was a little man very much at the mercy of both his wife and his daughter, and a prominent rôle at a wedding was not one he would look upon with favour. While Heather was placing a final spot of perfume behind her ears, ordering one of her golden curls that had escaped from under her chaplet of white roses, and picking up her white gloves from her dressing-table with a leisureliness that would almost certainly be maddening to the waiting man below, feeling further frustrated by morning clothes, the latter would almost certainly be taking a wistful peep at the dining-room sideboard, and wishing he might dare to fortify himself for his ordeal.

But he wouldn't dare to fortify himself with a quick whisky because Heather would already be descending the stairs and Rose—whose imagination was extraordinarily vivid today—could see her sweeping down them, in all the glory of her bridal white. Even her father would temporarily forget his nervousness and be a little overcome by the picture she made.

But, behind them in the church, the congregation was getting restless, and hymn sheets were rustling, and there was that curious whisper running through the church which was caused by women in rustling dresses moving slightly on hard pews, and heads being turned constantly to watch the door.

Rose, who had not so far succumbed to the desire to do so—although the other three bridesmaids were continually peeping in and whispering a little about the looks of the bridegroom and his best man, who was a close personal friend—suddenly found that she had to look in through the great Norman doorway and see how her guardian was taking this waiting — this somewhat protracted waiting.

She hadn't seen him since the afternoon before, and it seemed to her that there was little or no expression on his face as he stared down at the stone floor of the church, and waited for his bride to arrive. He was looking completely impeccable in his morning dress—but, then, he always looked impeccable in whatever he wore. He was naturally fastidious, and he paid his tailor a good deal to keep him looking a thoroughly well-dressed man.

In the sunshine that was once again streaming through the window above the altar his dark head looked very sleek, and although it was so dark there were a few burnished gleams caught up with the darkness. He had broad, well-held shoulders, narrow hips, and a kind of feline elegance. His square jaw looked very noticeable, and his lips were rather tightly compressed—which was the only sign of tension. He did not keep turning his head towards the door at the head of the aisle, although his best man did so constantly.

Rose felt, as she allowed herself to look thus deliberately on her guardain, that she was looking at him for the last time, in the sense that he would never again be quite the same man to her. He would be someone else's proprety—Heather's —and the pleasant relationship that had existed between them for the past five years would be over—severed because Heather would wish it so.

This might even be the last time she would actually have an opportunity to look at him! For once back at Farnhurst Manor she proposed to escape as quickly as possible to her own room.

Her heart seemed to swell with a kind of agony for a few moments as the realization rushed over her that parting—perhaps permanent parting!— was imminent. And then the fluttering, anxious movements of the other bridesmaids around her, the way in which they suddenly took to whispering, and then talking almost loudly, gradually penetrated to her consciousness, and she realized that the bride was very late indeed.

A couple of ushers joined them and stood talking in the porch. The people in the church behind grew ever more restless, and the bride's uncle— a stout gentleman on the Stock Exchange—who had been supporting Mrs. Willoughby, left his pew and made his appearance amongst both bridesmaids and ushers. As he did so the clock in the church tower chimed the hour—the bride was exactly half an hour late!

After that Rose was never exactly clear about what did happen. She only knew that she still stood there—beginning to shiver a little in her thin dress, because the sun didn't reach them in the grey stone porch, and the breeze was very persistent there in the shadows—and that her long, elbow-length lavender suede gloves began to feel very stiff, and the bunch of half-opened yellow roses curiously difficult to hold. One or two other relatives who felt they had a right to inquire what was going on emerged from the body of the church, and finally it was decided that a car must be sent back to find out what—if anything—had happened to the bride. Everybody insisted that nothing could have happened, that she was simply but unavoidably late, and that it was just possible her car had refused to start, and the chauffeur was having trouble with it. But, whatever was causing the delay, some inquiry concerning it must be made, for the bride's mother was already inclined to be a little overcome by agitation, and the vicar was only thinly disguising the fact that he had an urgent appointment in Rington at four o'clock. If the wedding was unreasonably delayed he might not be able to drive himself there in time.

Besides, there were all the other arrangements . . . The reception, the departure for the honeymoon . . . !

An usher suggested sensibly that the girls sat in one of the cars while they waited for the messenger to return from Farnhurst Manor, and when at last he did return there was no need for them to return to the church porch. The bride's note had only just been discovered by her father, who had not ventured to interrupt what he had believed was a somewhat protracted attention to the final details of her appearance until even his patience had worn thin, and then nothing but the note had awaited him on her dressing-table.

There was to be no wedding. The bride—or, that is to say, Heather, whom everyone had expected to become a bride that afternoon—had made other plans, and she and Peter Hurst were now on their way by road to a destination which Heather naturally hadn't disclosed in the brief note she left behind her.

When Rose found herself back at the Manor—with no knowledge of how Sir Laurence had reacted when the news had been broken to him—she was glad of the glass of sherry which someone thrust into her hand. She felt cold and bewildered, numb, tired and confused, and nothing any longer seemed completely real.

She had read of bridegrooms being jilted at the altar, but never, never had she dreamed that it would happen to her own Sir Laurence Melville.

CHAPTER V

THE next day she and Sir Laurence left Farn-hurst Manor and drove to Enderby.

Sir Laurence was very silent behind the wheel of the car, an unfamiliar, detached figure with a curiously emotionless mask of a face. It was rather like a granite mask, Rose thought, every time she found the courage to glance at it side-ways, and with nothing about it to encourage pleasantries. And as the journey was well over a hundred miles, and hardly any conversation took place while it lasted, the girl found it some-thing of a strain to say the least.

Not that she expected Sir Laurence to have much to say to her, or to anyone. His farewells at the Manor had been confined to his recent host and hostess—the latter all but prostrate in her own room—and he had ignored everybody else. The thing that amazed Rose was that, at such a time, he should remember her, and in-sist on carrying her away with him, although she had ventured to suggest that there was no need for him to bother about her just then, because she could become the guest of Mrs. Wilson-Plunk-ett. But he had simply said:

"Pack your things, and we'll leave immediately after breakfast."

And there had been that in his voice that had brooked no further argument.

Rose was so much more than merely shocked by the disastrous termination to a wedding-day that had dawned so brightly, and so secretly concerned for her guardian, that she had scarcely slept a wink the night before. The enormity of this thing that had happened had appalled her, as it had honestly appalled poor Mr. and Mrs. Willoughby.

43

They were left with all the presents to return and the bills to settle for a wedding that had never taken place, and with no financial reward or assistance to be looked for from a newly-acquired son-in-law. They weren't even sure that their daughter had so far acquired a husband, and that they wouldn't have to continue to be responsible for her maintenance, for Peter Hurst was by no means a man of substance.

In fact he was exactly the opposite.

Poor Mrs. Willoughby was literally drowned in tears when she said good-bye to Sir Laurence. It was only sheer desperation that provided her with sufficient courage to ask, just before he left:

"Of course, if, after all, Heather changed her mind—if nothing came of this dreadful elopement!—you would—take her back? Or wouldn't you?"

But Sir Laurence returned no answer at all to this, and cut short the embarrassing farewells. When he went out of the house Mrs. Willoughby felt sure she would never see him again.

Rose, full of deep, feminine compassion for that stony look in his face, would have been honestly glad if he had overlooked her on this occasion. She felt that she was just an unnecessary encumbrance to him, and that it was almost indecent that she should be thrust on him at such a time. Although, on the other hand, so rigid and inhuman was the exterior he was presenting to the world that she was glad that at least she was near enough to him to prevent him doing anything rash should the sudden impulse overwhelm him.

If it had been she, herself, who had been left standing at the altar . . . who had waited a full hour for a bridegroom who had never arrived at the church. . . . She was certain she would have wanted to crawl away and hide herself.

But men, perhaps, were different. Perhaps they reacted differently. . . .

When they arrived at Enderby, Thatcher, who had been sent on ahead, was there to receive them. He was looking unnaturally grave, and pointedly avoided lifting his eyes to his master's face. Rose felt certain that this was his way of attempting to deal tactfully with the situation.

Enderby was looking much as usual, and far nicer, Rose thought, than Farnhurst Manor. It was far more genuine than Farnhurst, for one thing, and Sir Laurence had filled it with costly treasures. There was nothing at all that jarred, and every evidence of a generous-sized bank-balance behind its owner. As she made her way up to her own room Rose wondered what it was that had affected Heather Willoughby, and caused her to behave as she had behaved. For she had sacrificed quite a lot. . . .

At dinner that night the oppressive silence in the dining-room pressed upon Rose like a living thing, and she wondered whether she wouldn't have been wiser to have pleaded some excuse for having a tray served to her in her room. Sir Laurence seemed hardly aware that she existed, and she was too terrified of saying the wrong thing to attempt any conversation on her own. It was not until the meal was practically over, and Thatcher had received instructions not to bother about serving coffee in the drawing-room, but to bring it straight to the dining-room that the man at the head of the table seemed to rouse himself deliberately from the close abstraction that had held him for more than twenty-four hours and looked across at his ward.

"I've brought you back here, Rose," he told her, "because we've got to decide something about your future. I'm going away almost immediately, so what would you like to do?"

"You're—going away?" Rose echoed, rather foolishly.

"Yes." He stared at her with a harsh, cool smile on his lips. "Does that surprise you so very

45

much? Did you imagine I was going to hang on here, or in London, surrounded by all my well-meaning friends, and receive their condolences?"

"I—I'm afraid I never thought of it—like that," she admitted.

"No." The almost hostile smile remained clinging about his shapely mouth. "I don't suppose you did. But, then, you haven't been jilted—to make use of a good old-fashioned expression—have you? So there's no reason why you should think about it."

Rose looked across the flower-decked table—it might have revealed greater tactfulness, she thought, on the part of Thatcher, if he had been content with a rather more restrained centre-piece; and to bring out such a blaze of silver as well-nigh dazzled the eyes seemed a little unnecessary for two people, dining together under such clouded circumstances—and allowed her gaze to rest with sudden quiet insight on her guardian's face. What had happened to him had no doubt been a severe shock, and beneath that harsh mask he must be suffering a good deal, but he was also seething with an anger greater than anything he had probably ever felt before in his life. It reminded her of the anger of a mortally hurt creature, and she realized it was capable of lashing out at her at any moment. And although she didn't in the least mind him losing his temper with her, because it no doubt helped him to vent it on someone, she did feel all at once the shadow of a bleak disappointment falling across her—she also felt suddenly intensely critical.

For if she, a mere nineteen-year-old, with little or no experience of Life, and Mrs. Wilson-Plunkett, with a vast deal of experience of Life, had both realized that Heather Willoughby was the last woman in the world he ought to marry, surely he might have had the sense to know it himself? To be—in a sense—prepared?

46

As Thatcher reappeared and set a coffee cup at her elbow, and then asked her in his perfect manservant manner whether she would like a liqueur, she waved him away with more impatience than she had probably allowed herself to display in her life before—certainly in front of her guardian.

"Will you allow me to say something?" she asked, very quietly.

Sir Laurence, waiting until he was quite sure Thatcher had retreated behind his green baize door, sent her a coldy derisive look.

"Certainly, my dear! Say what you want to say!"

"Then I hope you don't imagine that *I* wish to condole with you?"

"Don't you?" For the first time he noticed that she was looking rather white and strained, as if she had endured quite a lot herself since she returned from Switzerland. "Then what do you wish to do?" with great dryness.

"Tell you that I think you're lucky—yes, lucky! —to have escaped as you have!" She was aware that she had absolutely no right at all to say what she was saying, and that it was madness to do so, but once having started she had to go on. "Why you ever became engaged to Heather Willoughby I can't think—it was *obvious* she'd let you down! Even her own god-mother knew that! Probably her parents were afraid of it—but you were such a wonderful catch that they just prayed she wouldn't do anything foolish before the wedding! But she did!—she behaved dreadfully, and you're sitting there looking as if you've lost all faith in human nature. . . ."

Her voice died away as she saw that he had turned absolutely white, and his eyes were suddenly flaming at her—without any resemblance at all to the quiet grey eyes she had known for years. He stood up in his place at the table and

47

she had the feeling that he might actually strike her.

"How dare you?" he demanded, his voice trembling with a kind of cold fury. "How dare you talk to me like that?—and about the woman I was going to marry! And how dare you infer that you've discussed Heather and me with a talkative old harridan like that Mrs. Wilson-Plunkett . . .?"

"She's known Heather for years," Rose defended the only friend she had felt she had made during her short sojourn at Farnhurst Manor. "And at least she isn't blind! . . ." She, too, stood up at the opposite end of the table, and she knew she was trembling, and suddenly afraid—but her red hair refused to permit her to show any signs of it, or to haul down her flag. "And I've no doubt there were lots of other people who were not blind, either!"

He walked to the fireplace and turned and stood in the middle of the rug, looking at her as if she was a serpent he had never suspected he was harbouring in his bosom.

"How old are you?" he demanded icily.

"N-nineteen," she answered.

"And I suppose you think that nineteen years experience of life gives you the right to talk to me as if you were thirty-nine?"

"I haven't had any experience of life, but I—I . . ." Her throat went dry, and her voice trailed away. If only she could tell him about the night when she had discovered Heather in Peter Hurst's arms in the library—at a time when she was still obviously intending to go through with the wedding, for purely mercenary reasons — but she knew that she couldn't do that. Not even to support the strength of her own arguments, and make it seem less appalling that she was airing her opinions at all, could she do him further hurt, if that was possible.

48

"You what?" with almost brutal sarcasm.

"I felt doubtful about Heather from the beginning," rather feebly.

"You mean you disliked her?"

"No, I——"

"You disliked her and she disliked you, because she probably realized—as I never did—that in spite of all I've done for you you were an unnatural little hypocrite who wouldn't yield an inch."

"But that's not fair!" she gasped, taken completely aback. "I never showed my dislike!"

"Oh, yes, you did," with harsh grimness. "And you can't blame Heather if she resented it! She was prepared to accept you because you were my ward—be nice to you for my sake—but I realize now that you made it impossible for her to be that. She warned me about you—that you were the type to get the bit between your teeth and turn out to be ungrateful. But I wouldn't listen. I was constantly taking up the cudgels on your behalf, and because I did——"

"Because you did you lost Heather? Is that what you think?" Rose asked, with sudden, extraordinary calmness.

Sir Laurence had the grace to look faintly ashamed of himself—even doubtful and unsure of himself. And then, as he saw her large, extraordinarily clear green eyes watching him as if there was something about him that hypnotized her, he answered in a hard tone:

"There's no doubt about it, you complicated matters! After all, Heather isn't much older than you are, and I suppose I hadn't actually the right to expect her to look upon you as a kind of daughter. Naturally, she didn't like the idea of my having a ward at all."

"Then in that case, I—I'm sorry for having brought you so much unhappiness! If I'd known," in a strangled voice, "that I, and I alone, was going to be the cause of ruining everything for you, I'd never have come back to England at all! I

49

told you I didn't want you to have to go on being responsible for me, and now I—I'll go away at once. . . ."

"You'll do nothing of the kind," he said shortly, turning and staring at the logs that were smouldering on the wide hearth, for the October evening was chill. "*I'm* going away—right away!—and it needn't matter to anyone where I'm going! But you'll stay here with the housekeeper to look after you until you've made some plans, and your allowance will be paid to you regularly through my solicitors. Whatever you decide to do that allowance will continue, and when I get back—if you still feel that you want some sort of a career . . ."

"I don't want a career, and I don't want your money," she answered numbly. "But I'd like to go to bed now if I may."

"Of course." He turned, and all at once his voice was more gentle. "Rose, don't take to heart any of the things I've been saying! I'm—" he made a hopeless little gesture with his beautiful long-fingered hands—"I'm not quite myself, I suppose."

But sympathy for him seemed to have become frozen in her heart. She only felt that she wanted to get away from him—somewhere where she could stay away.

"Please," she repeated, "if you've no more to say I'd like to go upstairs. . . ."

"I won't keep you, child." He suddenly held out his hand to her. "I shall be gone in the morning, Rose. Let's part friends."

But as she put hers into it her finger-tips struck him as cold as ice. There was a blind, hurt look in her eyes which he remembered for a long time afterwards.

"Good-bye," she whispered. "And thank you for all you've—done for me!"

And then she fled from the room.

CHAPTER VI

Six months later, in the corridor of an express train which was carrying her to Rome, Rose was standing looking out of the window and enjoying the flying scenery when a young man emerged from a compartment behind her and stood lighting a cigarette and regarding her with interest.

Rose was not really aware of him, although she had heard the compartment door open and close. She was thinking how very fortunate—quite singularly fortunate—she was, to be on her way to the Eternal City, and a first visit to Italy after spending several weeks in Austria at a winter sports centre. And before that it had been Christmas in Northern Ireland with friends of Mrs. Wilson-Plunkett, and before that some extraordinarily pleasant and peaceful weeks at Mrs. Wilson-Plunkett's flat in London.

Rose was already sincerely attached to Mrs. Wilson-Plunkett, and there were occasions when she was quite sure she would end up by becoming extremely devoted to her. If one overlooked her slight eccentricities, her assumed cynicism—for at heart, Rose had discovered, she was an incurable romantic and extremely sentimental, hence the false curls and the clinging to girlish fripperies and lavish displays of jewellery—she was unusually kind and considerate, and very easy to get on with. While Rose was standing in the corridor, having expressed a desire to stretch her legs, she was dozing in their compartment after rather a heavy lunch, and occasional snores finding their way out into the corridor caused the girl to smile suddenly, and to turn and make certain that the compartment door was securely fastened so that others might not hear the slightly

51

discordant noises above the rattle of the train wheels.

It was then that she discovered the young man behind her, and flushed because he was unmistakably engrossed with her appearance.

"The lady with whom you travel is enjoying a siesta," he remarked, carrying his freshly-lighted cigarette to his lips and studying her over the glowing tip of it out of a pair of extraordinarily lustrous and quite remarkably handsome dark eyes. He was, she thought—feeling oddly startled by his nearness—the handsomest young man she had ever seen in her life, with an olive skin and amazingly long eyelashes and a graceful, slender build. She remembered catching a glimpse of him when he boarded the train at Verona that morning with an older man, and she had actually looked for him in the restaurant car at breakfast, although she wasn't quite certain why.

"Y-yes," she found herself stammering in answer. Then all at once she smiled naturally. "I'm afraid it's rather obvious, isn't it?"

The young man smiled back, quickly, flashingly. He had the whitest teeth and they were almost too faultlessly even.

"She is you duenna?" he inquired.

Rose shook her head.

"Oh, no." She wasn't quite certain how to describe Mrs. Wilson-Plunkett, since the old lady herself had forbidden her to proclaim to the world that she was her employer. And since she paid her a very generous salary for doing practically nothing, she certainly was an employer, although an extremely unusual one. "She is a—very dear friend," she concluded.

"Since you say so, *signorina*, I will accept it as nothing less than the truth, and a recommendation to get to know your very dear friend."

His smiling eyes were taking in the lovely golden tan she had acquired during recent weeks in the mountains, and the way her carnation

52

flush mounted beneath it. The splendour of her red curls had captivated him the instant he caught his first glimpse of her, and those hazel-green eyes were surprisingly shy for a young woman whose appearance was both *soignee* and sophisticated. He was not to know, of course, that the latter was due to Mrs. Wilson-Plunkett's insistence, before they left London, on spending a great deal of money on her latest diversion; but he was able to recognize the cut of expensive clothes, and grooming that was the result of a good deal of expenditure also.

"As a matter of fact," he admitted, as a slightly cool look overspread Rose's face, "my uncle, who is with me, is certain that he has seen your friend before."

"Oh!" Rose exclaimed.

"In fact, he's so certain that he is most anxious to recall himself to her memory."

Rose's delicate eyebrows arched.

"Then why doesn't he do so?"

"Because I promised to make certainty doubly certain by speaking to you on the subject first!"

His smile this time was tinged with apology because he realized that he was inviting a rebuff himself; but there was something about that smile, and the delightful deference in his voice, which prevented Rose from freezing him with a glance. Instead, when he threw his half-smoked cigarette out of the window, and then produced a gold case with some sort of a monogram engraved on it, and offered it to her, she accepted—a thing she would have declined to do six months before.

"Your—uncle?" she echoed, as he applied a gold lighter to the end of her cigarette.

"Prince Paul de Lippi. I am Camillo de Lippi." He introduced himself with an air of quiet grace, and apologized for not having done so immediately with even more courtly charm and correctness. "But I was a little diffident in approaching you, *signorina*, although the moment I caught sight of you on the platform this morning I knew that I had to know you," looking at her with somewhat disconcerting directness. "That is why it struck me as very fortunate that my uncle is so certain he and your friend are acquainted."

"But I don't think my friend is at all certain she is acquainted with your uncle," Rose murmured, a little awkwardly.

"And the name of your friend?"

"Mrs. Wilson-Plunkett."

"Ah! Then it is so!" He sounded vastly relieved. "Mrs. Wilson-Plunkett is the sister of the Marchesa de Cantonelli, and the two ladies are so much alike that one could pass easily for the other. My uncle has known the Marchesa for many years, but your Mrs. Wilson-Plunkett he has not met for quite a long while. Therefore you will understand that he could not be absolutely sure he was not making a mistake."

"Yes," Rose agreed, "I do see that."

"And," with unmistakable eagerness, "may I take it that you are on your way to stay with the Marchesa in Rome?"

"Well, no," Rose replied to this, "I'm afraid we aren't. At least—the Marchesa is in America at the moment, receiving treatment for a rheumatic condition, but if she returns before we leave we shall probably visit her. And, as a matter of fact, she has offered her villa to Mrs. Wilson-Plunkett if she cares to stay in it."

"But for a while at least you will be staying in a hotel?"

Rose nodded.

"Then that is almost as good!" The dark eyes positively sparkled. "And you will permit me to see something of you—?"

A sudden tapping on the glass window of the compartment behind her, indicating that Mrs. Wilson-Plunkett was awake, saved Rose the necessity for committing herself one way or the other, and the young man hastened away to return with his uncle, Prince Paul de Lippi. Although a good many years older than his nephew, the prince had as much silken-voiced charm as Camillo, and in spite of the fact that there were touches of pure white in his night-dark hair at the temples, he was almost as startlingly handsome. And the poise and polish his extra years had bestowed on him commended him very favourably to Rose.

Mrs. Wilson-Plunkett, too, seemed delighted to renew an acquaintance that she had all but forgotten, and when they arrived in Rome there was no question of taking a taxi to their hotel. A beautiful Italian car, pale ivory and black, glittering with chromium fittings, in the charge of a liveried chauffeur, awaited the de Lippi uncle and nephew, and Rose found herself sharing the back seat with her employer and Camillo, while Prince Paul occupied the seat beside the driver in front.

The journey to the hotel seemed to pass in a flash—although they climbed one of the Seven Hills of Rome while it lasted—and Rose was a little disappointed because her first impressions of the Eternal City were a little confused. Normally she would have looked about her eagerly, following their arrival in the extremely modern and impressive great railway station. But with Camillo's dark, absorbed eyes on her face she felt constrained to keep her enthusiasm in check, at any rate until she was free to indulge it without every excited turn of her red head being so closely observed.

Nevertheless, she was aware of warm spring sunshine, turning a little red because the afternoon was near its close, falling across magnificent streets and squares, and fountains sparkling like diamonds in the arrestingly beautiful light. There seemed to be domes and cupolas and arches soaring into the unclouded blue of the sky on all sides of her, and just before the car decanted them outside the hotel Camillo pointed out to her the dome of St. Peter's, rising out of the thirteen-acre Vatican city which, she was to discover later, was an independent state, without any visible barriers to exclude the curious. In fact—and this, too, she was to discover later—there were three Romes: Ancient, Modern and Papal, and all three had an overwhelming amount to offer to someone who had never seen anything like them before.

Just before the car drove off again, and their luggage was carried into the hotel, Camillo bent over Rose's hand and saluted it in a fashion which for an instant surprised her so much that she almost instinctively pulled her hand away. And then, when he looked into her eyes in the dying light and murmured: "I shall see you soon again, *signorina*'" she felt herself blushing absurdly, and was conscious of a curious sensation on the backs of her fingers where a handsome pair of masculine lips had pressed themselves for a moment, and left, as it were, an imprint.

She was not at all sure whether she approved of the sensation or not.

Inside the hotel, with its lights and its flowers and its atmosphere of almost oppressive luxury, Mrs. Wilson-Plunkett pulled off her hat before ever the lift had carried them to the suite reserved for them—for somehow such matters as currency never seemed to cause any serious inconvenience to the wealthy widow, who had financial interests, Rose surmised, in a good many countries—and announced that now they had arrived in Rome she was going to rest. She rang the bell for tea to be brought to them and a chambermaid to unpack their things, and then sank down in a comfortable chair and looked at Rose with a twinkle of amusement in her eyes.

"But you, my dear, will not be dull," she said. "Not unless that young man with the extraordinary eyelashes is unlike every member of his family I've ever known or heard of!"

"What do you mean?" Rose inquired, feeling oddly embarrassed as she poured out the tea.

56

"Have they some sort of a peculiarity as a family?"

"Not at all, my dear," with a definitely amused smile. "But they do have what is known as an 'eye' for a pretty face—the male members, of often told you. And Camillo recognized that immediately. He'll see to it that you get to know Rome very well indeed!"

But when Rose finally went to her own room to change for the evening it was not of Camillo de Lippi she was thinking as she stood before her handsomely-curtained window and looked out at a crescent moon climbing into a tender sea of blue above the misty towers of Rome. She was thinking of another man of whom she had heard nothing at all in the past six months, and wondering in which corner of the globe he was wandering at that moment, and whether the same crescent moon was by any chance shining down on him.

Mrs. Wilson-Plunkett's statement that Rose would not be allowed to be dull, although she herself proposed to rest for a while after their journey from Austria, was proved to be entirely correct in the next few days. Camillo de Lippi gave Rose twenty-four hours to get her bearings, as it were, and then descended on her and the hotel in a rakish-looking bright blue sports type of car, and offered to show her anything and everything that she wished to see.

In his company Rose made the acquaintance of the Colosseum, and sat in the forum with a guidebook on her knees and tried to re-create for herself the wonders of that world of Ancient Rome which are now no more than pages of passionate history. She visited St. Peter's and the gorgeous Sistine Chapel, which took away her breath with its lasting testimonials to the brilliance of Raphael and Michelangelo. Her eyes were dazzled by the splendour of the Papal Guard, and enchanted by the doves fluttering down from the shadows of the mighty church to search for crumbs between the feet of the passers-by, while the sunlight fell with a kind of white-hot brilliance, although it was only spring. She visited each of the fountains in turn —because for some reason they fascinated her more than anything else in Rome—and dropped a coin into the famous Fountain de Trevi, which would ensure for her, Camillo assured her, a return to Rome.

"To fail to drop a coin into the Fountain de Trevi is as good as an admission that you do not wish to return to Rome," he added as he watched her bending eagerly above the marble basin and studying the coins that already lay there in the crystal-clear water.

"Then I must certainly drop one in," she replied, smiling up at him, "because I'm in love with it already!"

"Make a wish," he said suddenly as she extracted a lira from her purse and poised it between thumb and finger.

Rose looked surprised.

"If I do, is it likely to come true?"

"Of course—just as you will be certain to return to Rome!"

So she closed her eyes and wished and dropped her coin into the marble basin, and when she opened her eyes again Camillo was smiling at her.

"Although I'm not entitled to one, I do most earnestly wish that yours will come true," he told her, his dark eyes caressing her.

Rose for an instant had a faintly wistful air about her.

"It was quite a simple wish," she said. "It could come true."

But she didn't add that she hardly expected it to do so.

Camillo took her to lunch at one of Rome's most

exclusive restaurants, introduced her to some very smart young members of Roman Society, and begged permission to take her and Mrs. Wilson-Plunkett the opera. But sticking to her resolution to rest for a while, Mrs. Wilson-Plunkett declined the invitation for herself, while insisting that Rose would be delighted. And Rose wore a white lace dress that had been specially designed for her in London, and spent a somewhat unreal evening in an atmosphere of other far more splendid dresses and glittering displays of jewellery, and was afterwards entertained to supper in a very up-to-date night club, and driven home through the soft warmth of the Roman night with the feeling that she ought to be grateful for such an attentive escort.

There was another night when Mrs. Wilson-Plunkett, feeling more refreshed, accepted an invitation for herself as well as Rose to dine at Prince Paul de Lippi's villa, and on that occasion Rose wore drifting leaf-green chiffon, and Mrs. Wilson-Plunkett looked magnificent in black velvet and diamonds. The villa was situated on the heights above the town, was filled with costly treasures of period furniture, and some priceless collections of china and glass—for the prince, a wealthy man, was well known as a collector, and all sorts of *objets d'art* appealed to him—and surrounded by a garden that was like a garden in a fairy tale. There were slender pencil-like cypress trees, etched like black silhouettes against the starry night sky, terraces of silvery olives, paved walks bordered by exotic shrubs, and exquisite statuary. Rose was enchanted by it, and the host was delightful. His nephew paid her such exaggerated compliments that they frequently embarrassed her, but Prince Paul was more old-world in his attentiveness, very gentle and full of undeniable charm.

She was not surprised, when she learned from Mrs. Wilson-Plunkett that he was a widower, to learn also that he was very much sought after by mothers with marriageable daughters and by ambitious widows and ladies who could not rightly describe themselves as widows. In fact, both he and his nephew were immensely popular, and were seldom allowed a dull moment whenever they returned to Rome.

"We simply must return the courtesy and invite them both to dine with us," Mrs. Wilson-Plunkett said after the night at the villa.

And that was how it came about that, less than a fortnight after her arrival in Rome, Rose found herself dancing one evening in the cleared space in the magnificent dining-room of the hotel where they were staying, being expertly piloted by Camillo, while his uncle and Mrs. Wilson-Plunkett sat at a flower-decked table on the fringe of the floor and watched them moving very harmoniously together.

Camillo looked down at Rose's russet-hued head with unmistakable admiration in his handsome dark eyes, and the skirts of her white lace dress floated out behind her. Other eyes watched them, apart from the two pairs that had a right to be interested in their movements, and one pair of hitherto rather bored masculine grey ones developed a sudden, rather startled look of amazement in them as the lovely girl and the striking young man passed within a few feet. His companion, an exotic-looking woman of somewhat uncertain years, magnificently dressed, arched her brows for an explanation as he followed the progress of the pair.

"Is it that you know that young woman with the red hair, or are you perhaps acquainted with Prince Paul de Lippi's nephew?"

Although she spoke English beautifully, she had an unmistakable soft Italian accent, and there was a quality of silken smoothness in her voice as she put the question. There was an expression on her face as she watched the Englishman who was sharing her table that was rather reminiscent of a cat watching a bowl of cream it had earmarked for its own consumption.

Sir Laurence Melville's frown grew.

"And who is Prince Paul de Lippi?"

"Oh, a very charming man, a very wealthy man —that is him over at that table on the other side of the floor, with the very old lady with the dyed curls."

Sir Laurence looked and recognized Mrs. Wilson-Plunkett.

"What is wrong?" his companion asked, still more softly. "You look as if you are quite annoyed!"

"I am," Sir Laurence returned rather shortly, and crushed out his cigarette in the ash-tray.

It was at that moment that Rose, listening to Camillo telling her that although her eyes were almost green they reminded him, for some reason, of violets hidden in a bed of fern, moved her head a little restlessly, and looking deliberately away from the dark eyes above her encountered those of the man she had looked upon for the last five years as her guardian. She was so surprised that she instantly muffed her footsteps, Camillo found himself treading on one of her dainty silver sandals, apologized profusely, and then came to a standstill as he saw that she was scarcely attending.

"Is anything wrong?" he asked as he saw her eyes were wide and that she was staring as if hypnotized over his shoulder.

"No—no . . ." she answered, told herself that it must be the effect of the single glass of champagne she had drunk at dinner, and that she was imagining things; and then, without quite realizing what she was doing, looked in an entirely opposite direction.

Camillo swung her once more into the sensuous rhythm of the tango the orchestra was playing, holding her very closely because for a few moments it had seemed to him that she had ceased to be aware of him altogether. He guided her once more partly round the glistening floor, and then when the music suddenly came to an end and everyone clapped with Latin enthusiasm, led her back to their table, and Rose sank down in her place with the feeling that she simply dared not look again into the corner of the room where a man who looked like Sir Laurence was seated.

For it simply could not be Sir Laurence, sharing a table with a dark-haired tempestuous-looking Italian beauty who had actually had a hand resting caressingly on his arm!

"Bravo!" the prince exclaimed, diverting her for a moment. "You dance in a way that is a delight to watch, *signorina*, and if I were a little more skilled in these modern dances I would beg you to accept me as a partner. But as it is, I think you had better stick to Camillo," smiling at her.

Rose was only vaguely aware of how the rest of the evening passed, but she knew that she danced several more dances with Camillo, and that each time they drew near that end of the room where she was certain eyes still watched her, she rigidly refrained from looking where every instinct urged her to look. She grew mildly footsore, and rather tired, and the great room seemed to her to become oppressively warm, and at last Camillo whisked her out into the coolness of a huge glassed-in veranda. He placed her in a comfortable basket chair beside an open section of the glass, and then suggested fetching her something reviving to drink. As she accepted gratefully and smiled up to him, he lightly touched a loosened tendril of her hair, smiled back with that strong suspicion of an actual caress in his eyes, and then left her alone for the first time that evening.

And she was so grateful to be alone that she could almost have sighed with relief. It was one thing, she decided, as she lay back limply in the chair and felt the cool air fan her face, to be admired openly and treated like something rare and exotic—the spray of pure white orchids, for instance, attached to the front of her off-the-shoulder gown, which had arrived in cellophane for her that afternoon, with Camillo's card enclosed —for a short time. But for any length of time it became a little exhausting, especially as she was not yet accustomed to masculine admiration— certainly not masculine admiration backed by Italian ardour.

She liked Camillo immensely, and she wondered whether he treated all his girl friends to such an excess of devotion in the first few weeks after making their acquaintance, but she felt a little unable to cope with it tonight. And she wanted to think about the strange coincidence of that pair of eyes in the dining-room . . .

She had felt them following her progress before ever she suddenly turned her head and met their full regard, and in spite of surprise she had been certain immediately that she was looking into the eyes of Sir Laurence.

But lighting effects, warm air—that single glass of champagne—could have something to do with creating an illusion. Sir Laurence, even if he was in Rome, would not surely be consoling himself after six months with an obvious beauty like that brilliant-eyed Italian woman who had so possessively grasped at the sleeve of his dinner-jacket?

And then slow, rather measured, footsteps sounded behind her, and she turned. A voice—

very dry and masculine and measured also, and cold like the drip of ice—addressed her:

"So nowadays you don't recognize me when we meet, Rose? Such a lot of water has flowed underneath the bridge since that last night at Enderby that you prefer to forget about me altogether!"

CHAPTER VII

ROSE deserted her chair so swiftly and with such a startled movement that to an onlooker complete surprise would have been immediately deduced from her action. But it would have been a mistaken deduction, for although the sound of that well-remembered voice falling so suddenly on her ears did actually take her so much aback that she even turned a little white, she knew that she had been subconsciously waiting for it for very nearly a full hour. Ever since she had danced a tango with Camillo de Lippi.

"Perhaps," Sir Laurence suggested, his lips thin and curving a little bleakly—a kind of wintry half-smile—in the discreetly veiled light in the veranda, "you really did fail to recognize me when you and your Italian admirer passed close to my table in the dining-room? In which case six months must have altered me a good deal—just as they have most decidedly altered you!"

Rose put both hands up to her throat and clutched instinctively, with embarrassed fingers, at the single row of pearls that encircled it.

"I couldn't believe that it—that it was you," she said after striving to find a voice.

"Because I really have altered?"

"No; of course not," the words coming more rapidly. But in the dim light, rendered a little unnatural by the brilliance of the stars that seemed to be hanging close above the earth outside, he actually did strike her as being thinner, with a sharper line to his features, and one or two rather more noticeable silvery threads in his crisp brown hair at the temples. "But I wasn't expecting to—to see you so suddenly . . . And you were not alone . . ."

"Neither were you," he murmured. "And I wasn't expecting to see you at all—with or without an escort!"

"Signor de Lippi is a friend of Mrs. Wilson-Plunkett."

"And you have attached yourself to that good lady in the capacity of a long-lost daughter, or something of the sort?"

"I am her—her companion. She employs me."

"The sort of employment a good many young women of your age would like to obtain, I feel sure," he remarked, his eyes resting cynically on the pale perfection of her gown, and the spray of white orchids attached like butterflies' wings to the creamy warmth of one of her bare shoulders. "How much do you receive a week for services that have already struck me as quite unusually light?"

Rose moistened lips that had gone suddenly absolutely dry—not so much as a result of nervousness as shock, because he was suddenly standing there before her in the flesh, after she had dreamed about him and thought about him so often in the six months during which she had had no idea at all where he was, or what he was doing, but because it was plain he was still actively hostile towards her. His eyes looked bleak and hard and cold—not even with that slight softening he had introduced into them that last night at Enderby, when he had said that they must part friends. And trying to think up something to say to him to explain away her deceptive appearance of affluence—for she *was* no more than a companion really, and she did try to do everything in her power to merit the definitely quixotic generosity of a possibly whimsical old woman—her own eyes grew large and dark and abashed, and if anything her face grew paler with a sudden keen anxiety to convince him of her natural integrity.

"I had to do something," she said quickly, "and

Mrs. Wilson-Plunkett wanted me to live with her—"

"Sit down," he interrupted rather harshly, "and never mind Mrs. Wilson-Plunkett just now. Your Adonis friend will be returning very soon, I expect, with whatever refreshment he has gone to fetch for you, and I had to let you know that I had seen you. Why haven't you drawn your allowance during the last six months?"

"I had never any intention of drawing it," she replied, glad to sink down once again into the basket-chair she had so recently vacated, because for some reason her limbs were trembling a little, and the suddenness of the meeting had caused her heart to pound rather heavily. "That is to say, I had never any intention of drawing it after—"

"After I spoke to you in a way you were quick to resent?"

"No"—flushing rather painfully—"after I left Gerhardt. I planned to earn my own living once I left school."

"And that's what you're doing now?"

"I—yes. I haven't any need to draw any sort of an allowance."

"But what if there hadn't been any Mrs. Wilson-Plunkett? Would you have thrown yourself on the mercy of your Paris friends?"

"I might."

"Rather than continue to look upon me as a guardian with a right to support you?"

"You never had any right to support me—I mean, I never had any right to expect you to support me . . ."

A shadow approached them from the far end of the veranda, and when it drew nearer Rose saw that it was the elegant Italian woman of uncertain years. As she drew really close the younger girl could make out the dark exclusiveness of her dress, scattered all over with sequins, so that she shone like a myriad fireflies in the gloom. And against the shadowy darkness her skin looked matt and white as milk, her hair as dark as ebony, her mouth a scarlet lacquered flower. She smiled, and her teeth were small and perfect, her eyes disturbingly lustrous.

"I came in search of you, Lance," she said, slipping a hand inside his arm, "because it seemed that you were a long time away. Is this the little red-head who is your ward?"

Rose was conscious of a shiver of distate passing through her. So he had discussed her with this woman who had a Mona-Lisa-ish smile, and whose voice was drawling and a trifle mocking!

Sir Laurence made the necessary introduction formally.

"Rose, this is Signora Bardoli. I have already explained to her our relationship. Lola—Rose Hereward!"

"I am delighted to know you, little English Rose," Lola Bardoli said very softly, but Rose was quite sure she mocked as she held out a be-ringed hand. "Although I would not say that you are very typically English. With that hair, those eyes, and that skin"—the lustrous eyes flickering over them in turn—"you are just that little bit too exotic! Like a rare plant!"

Rose said nothing, and Sir Laurence's brows set in a quite noticeable frown.

"Rose," he said quickly, "will you tell Mrs. Wilson-Plunkett that I would be glad if she would see me tomorrow about twelve o'clock? And tell her also that if she will not lunch with me I shall expect you to do so!"

Rose stammered something about being willing to convey the message, and then added rather foolishly:

"I suppose, then, that you are—that you are staying in Rome? We had—we had no idea . . ."

Signora Bardoli laughed softly.

"A guardian and a ward who know nothing about each other's movements! Oh, Lance," looking up at him with a good deal of amusement in her eyes, "where is your sense of responsibility? Miss Hereward does strike me as being a little too emancipated to need a guardian——one who is not any older than you are, anyway!——but you should keep an eye on her, you know."

To Rose's relief, they were joined at that moment by Camillo, full of apologies for having taken some time in obtaining her drink, and more introductions took place. Rose thought that Sir Laurence looked with even greater bleakness in his eyes at the young and beautifully mannered Italian than had been noticeable in the grey depths when he looked at her, and she introduced him simply as Sir Laurence Melville, and not as anyone who had a right to interfere with any part of her life.

When he and the *signora* had left the veranda, Camillo looked after them with a faint, casual smile in his eyes.

"Very English!" he commented, plainly referring to Sir Laurence. "I have a feeling that he did not quite take to me, somehow. And the Signora Bardoli is not his type. But that," looking down at Rose in his caressing fashion, "is his affair, isn't it?"

When Mrs. Wilson-Plunkett received Sir Laurence's message she exclaimed impatiently:

"Bother the man for turning up just now! What on earth brings him to Rome? Tell him I'm not at my best these days, Rose, and that I have to rest a good deal. But if you have to lunch with him alone, don't let him bully you! You have told me he isn't your legal guardian, and he has forgotten all about you for six months, so he can go on forgetting about you."

"But he did make financial arrangements for me," Rose felt forced to defend Sir Laurence. "I would have been quite secure, even if you hadn't been so terribly kind."

"Rubbish, child!" the old lady exclaimed, recalling the dazed manner in which Rose had arrived at her London flat when she admitted that she had all but run away from Enderby after the disastrous breakdown to Sir Laurence's marriage. "You know very well you wouldn't have touched his money, and there is more to being a guardian than just providing a roof over your head. And if Sir Laurence had had any sense in the beginning he would never have got himself mixed up with Heather Willoughby, and there would never have been any jilting at the altar, or any necessity for him to disappear as he did—in a typically selfish, masculine fashion!—and forget every obligation he had undertaken."

Rose said nothing to this, but she still could feel nothing but sympathy for Sir Laurence because he had had to endure what he had had to endure, and she knew that she had never been a real obligation of his. He had been kind to her, and generous—far kinder, and far more generous than she had ever had any right to expect him to be—and she exonerated him completely from having failed her in any sense of the word as a guardian.

When he arrived at the hotel at twelve o'clock she was waiting for him in the main entrance lounge. She was wearing an oatmeal silk suit with a thickly-pleated skirt, and her hair was curling softly and vividly under a tiny brown velvet Juliet cap. Her accessories were all perfect—hand-made snakeskin shoes, with very high heels, a hand-bag that matched them, and suede gloves that emphasized the smallness and shapeliness of her hands.

Sir Laurence looked down at her for a moment as if he was deliberately taking in every detail of her appearance, and then remarked with an odd smile curving his lips:

"Why did I never realize before that you must be one of the loveliest young women in the world, Rose? Or did it take Mrs. Wilson-Plunkett's genius to bring out the best in you?"

Rose returned no answer to this but her heart was beating more quickly than normally as she accompanied him from the hotel, and she was glad that he didn't seem greatly to mind when she explained about Mrs. Wilson-Plunkett. She had the feeling that eyes watched them as they left the hotel, and she realized that her escort looked extremely distinguished — and no doubt "very English" in the eyes of observant Romans— dressed in his usual impeccable fashion, and in spite of the fact that he was definitely thinner and older-looking than six months ago, with something about him that attracted glances like a magnet. Especially, Rose noted, feminine glances.

She decided that it was his experiences—or the lingering effects of one bitter experience—over the past six months which had lent him that look of cool aloofness and faint hardness, as well as a certain cynical detachment, which he had never noticeably worn before.

"Where would you like to go?" he asked when he had hailed a taxi. "Have you tried one of the open-air restaurants yet? If not, it might be a change for you."

His tone suggested that as she probably enjoyed a good many fresh experiences these days he was not expecting her to show enthusiasm; but when they were seated beneath the pergola of an open-air restaurant that was obviously very popular, judging by the well-filled tables, he noticed that her transparent and extraordinarily beautiful greenish eyes brightened as if the novelty appealed to her a good deal. Apart from that, she was looking rather pale, and the uncertain movements of her hands indicated a state of nervousness. He was not to know that she had slept very little the night before because, after weeks of putting him as much as possible out of her thoughts, and having nothing to remind her of him, his sudden reappearance in a part of the world where she had never dreamed of meeting him had affected her like a harsh coming face to face with realities.

All night she had tossed restlessly and heard him accusing her of being the cause of the breakdown of his marriage plans, and all night she had felt shaken because a man in whom she had placed absolute trust had turned and regarded her as if she was a viper he had suddenly discovered he was nursing in his bosom. And although he had apologized afterwards she knew that the apology could never mean very much.

The old relationship between them was at an end. And she had dressed that morning with a dread of meeting him again, although something deep down inside her had looked forward pathetically to the meeting.

"Rose," he said suddenly, after studying her face rather intently for several seconds and realizing that she deliberately avoided any direct contact with his eyes, "I'm more than sorry about that last night at Enderby. I'm afraid I said something very unpleasant to you, and it wasn't in the least true."

Rose, with a wine-glass half-way to her lips, felt her hand tremble, and she set it down again.

"You were very upset," she said mechanically. "And you probably thought it was true at the time."

He smiled suddenly with a touch of the old sweetness.

"Poor little Rose! Of course there was no shadow of excuse for what I said!"

72

"Well—it doesn't matter now." She looked down at the wine in her glass, and he thought how delectable the shadow of her long eyelashes was on her creamy cheeks. "All that is—well, it belongs to the past, doesn't it?"

"Does it?"

"Yes. Yes, of course." She took a hasty sip at her wine and hoped he didn't notice that her hand was still unsteady. "I hope that in future everything will be—well, very much happier for you, and that you won't need ever to recall that last night at Enderby."

He was silent for a few moments, while the waiter provided a fresh course. And then, when the man had disappeared he said:

"I haven't been back to Enderby since October, but it never occurred to me that you would rush away from it, too."

"I don't think you were in a state of mind at that time to care very much what I did," she remarked, staring at the spaghetti in front of her and hoping she didn't sound as if she was accusing him of turning his back on his obligations. And in order to correct such an impression if she had created one she added: "But of course I understood the state of mind you were in."

"Did you? Did you, Rose?" looking at her through darkened and suddenly inscrutable eyes. "I hope you never understand quite such a state of mind as that!"

Rose attacked the spaghetti and felt that it would choke her, in spite of the fact that it was superbly cooked and known locally to be incomparable, as all the misery and tension of that last dreadful day at Farnhurst Manor washed over her.

"When you marry, Rose," Sir Laurence addressed his own heaped plateful of food, with an expression on his face which suggested he expected it to turn to dust and ashes in his mouth, "you must be very, very careful to pick someone who will never under any circumstances let you down! Very, very careful!" he repeated.

Rose returned no answer to this, and he twirled the stem of his wineglass thoughtfully, his eyes returning to her as if she was a magnet that drew them.

"But you're young yet," he remarked, studying the delicate outline of her face, the sensitive, vulnerable lines of her soft mouth, and the strength of the little chin below it. "Much too young even to be thinking of marriage for years yet."

And then he saw how the eyes of a couple of dark-haired young men near to them were watching her, recalled the look in the handsome eyes of Prince Paul de Lippi's nephew the night before, when Rose had been closely held in his arms—the graciousness of the prince himself when the girl returned to her table—and felt himself frowning suddenly.

"Don't you agree with me, Rose?"

"I"—Rose looked up and met his eyes directly for the first time—"I haven't really thought about such things—not seriously," she admitted. And then she rushed on: "But I would like to know something about you—how you—you've been getting on all this long time. Naturally, I've thought about you ..." That, she could have told him, was a vast understatement. "You were always very kind to me, and I suppose I've worried about you, too."

"That, Rose," he told her with a gentleness that could have overlaid a certain mockery, "was very good and feminine of you!"

She tried not to look abashed, although she had to lower her eyes before the undisguised mockery in his.

"I've wondered whether—whether you were travelling about very much. It's quite a long time —six months ..."

74

"It is," he agreed very quietly. "And I have travelled quite a bit—here, there and everywhere!" His bleak smile did not suggest that he had enjoyed himself. "But at least I've been diverted, and now I'm in Rome I'm thinking of getting down to some serious work again. A friend of mine has lent me his flat, and it's very comfortable, and I think I can work there very well. The architecture of this city intrigues me—both the old and the new. The old seems to be practically imperishable, and the new could blend with it so much less harmoniously than it actually does do."

Rose agreed with him with sudden enthusiasm, and they talked for a while of Rome in voices that were more or less normal, and the girl felt a little of the tension die out of her as she discovered that they both shared a great deal of admiration for the city of the Cæsars. Bnt then he asked her how long she had been in the Italian capital, and what she had been doing before that, and when she told him about Austria and the visit to Ireland before that, she saw him smile a little enigmatically.

"You've suddenly become a very travelled young woman, Rose," he told her. "I'll confess that when I saw you last I didn't think your emancipation was going to be so sudden—or so complete!" his eyes taking in all the perfection of her beautifully fitting silk suit, and everything else calculated to arouse admiration about her. "Before, you were a very charming nineteen-year-old who had just said good-bye to her finishing school, and had no real plans for the future—now you're a completely finished product, devastatingly attractive—if you'll permit a mere ex-guardian to make the observation!—and all as the result of a little expenditure by a very wealthy old woman! Is she going to adopt you, Rose?"

Rose shook her head instantly.

"Of course not!"

"Marry you off, then, to someone as wealthy as herself? And take to herself all the credit for doing so!"

Again Rose said "Of course not!" but her face flamed a little.

Sir Laurence's now very cynical gaze continued to rest on her.

"You're a beauty, Rose, and you'll no doubt cause a lot of havoc amongst masculine hearts before you've finished. But I strongly recommend you not to be carried away by the ardour and admiration of young men like the younger de Lippi, with whom you were dancing last night. His uncle is a man of substance, and unimpeachable reputation, and a different proposition altogether; but from the little I've been able to gather about Camillo in a matter of a few hours there is nothing to indicate that he will ever be a man of substance also. He isn't even his uncle's heir, although supported by him for the time being—so don't take him too seriously, will you?"

"I don't know what you mean," Rose said, flushing again, and rather more wildly than before.

"Don't you? Then I'll put it into simple language for you," Sir Laurence replied, leaning across the table towards her and gently touching one of her hands. "Young men like Camillo de Lippi are not exactly two a penny in Rome, but there are a great many of them, and most of them are looking for wealthy wives. It would be a pity if this young man got the wrong ideas about you—and the relationship in which you stand to Mrs. Wilson-Plunkett!"

For an instant Rose's embarrassment was almost painful and then she got the better of it, and a feeling of anger and resentment took possession of her.

"I don't think," she said, her voice quivering a little as it had quivered once before when she had found the courage to stand up to him and say things she had felt very strongly at the time ought to be said to him by someone, "that you have any right at all to try and turn me against the friends I have made. *Or* to make inquiries about them for the purpose of turning me against them! And even if Camillo de Lippi were not my friend—and *nothing* more!—you would still have no right to under-value him in anyone's eyes!"

"Touché", Sir Laurence exclaimed, and gave her fingers a firm, hard squeeze. "You once told me that I ought to have had more sense—or you inferred it!—at my age than to pick upon a woman to marry who would let me down in the worst possible fashion, and I'll admit I was surprised at the time. In fact, I was astonished! But now I've returned the compliment by expressing my belief in *your* having more sense—although you're not much more than a babe in arms compared with my advanced years!—than to allow yourself to succumb to Italian flatteries which might lead nowhere. And I'm not under-valuing the looks of that so obvious admirer of yours!"

There was a faintly rueful expression in his eyes, as well as a kind of earnest desire that she should not altogether decline to listen to him. She said quickly:

"I know I owe you an apology for the things I said to you that night. You were upset—I hadn't any right to attack you as I did!"

"On the contrary, I found what you said distinctly salutary." But the faint smile in his eyes was still rather more disturbing than rueful. "And, Rose, I haven't any intention of relinquishing the right to keep an eye on you, so I'm afraid you'll have to go on looking upon me as an unofficial guardian. I don't turn my back on responsibilities, and I promised your father I'd look after you."

"But he hadn't any right to expect you to do so." She collected her handbag and gloves as he looked towards the waiter and demanded their bill. "And as far as I'm concerned," not meeting his eyes, but feeling quite determined nevertheless, "in future I intend to be entirely responsible for my own actions!"

His smile was unusually quizzical as he followed her out from under the pergola and into the almost blinding sunshine.

As they subsided on the back seat of a taxi he asked:

"Are you in a rush to get back, Rose? Is your Mrs. Wilson-Plunkett a slave-driver?"

"Of course not." Rose denied the charge almost indignantly. "She's terribly kind to me."

"That was the impression I had rather gathered," he admitted, with another dry look at her clothes. "Then in that case can you spare me a little more of your time and let me show you a wonderful view?"

"I'd love to see it—if *you've* got the time to spare for me!"

She meant it, and in fact her heart almost leapt at the thought that she would not have to say good-bye to him again for a little while longer. For, once she said good-bye to him, who knew when she would see him again?

But he sent her another quizzical look.

"That was rather an edged reply of yours, Rose —or ought I to address you as Miss Hereward now that our relations are a little different?"

"Don't be absurd, Sir Laurence," she answered quickly.

"*Sir* Laurence? It used to be Lance!"

She smiled at him a little mistily—or that was the impression her limpid green eyes managed to convey in the gloom of the taxi—and with a great deal of the old Rose simplicity and rather shy contentment.

"Thank you very much, Lance, for taking me out to lunch," she said, with the same shy simplicity in her voice. "It was something I—didn't expect this time yesterday!"

CHAPTER VIII

THE view he wanted to show her was certainly breath-taking, but before she could see it she had to allow him to escort her into the lift which served several floors of a handsome block of very up-to-date flats, and on the top floor he opened the door of his own flat and led her into it. She looked about her in delight at the airiness of his sitting-room, with its extreme air of comfort and almost lavish furnishings, and then followed him out on to the balcony on to which the windows of the room gave.

"There! You see what I mean, Rose?" Sir Laurence demanded as he waved a hand to indicate the view. "The whole of Rome spread out before you! Rather like being up in an aircraft, isn't it?"

Rose clutched the balcony rail excitedly, and agreed that it was.

Although the height was not really great, there was a sensation of being elevated in space, and in the sparkling warmth of the afternoon she could see Rome in its entirety, with its towers and its campaniles shimmering against the backcloth of the Latium hills and the Alban mountains. And in spite of the warmth there was all the freshness and tenderness of spring in the air, and she could almost smell the flower-filled gardens of the *palazzos* and villas that were so much a part of the beauty of Rome, and the hot scent of the olives that crowned the slopes.

"I've been here about three weeks now," Sir Laurence said, "and I've decided that I shall never grow tired of this view."

"I don't think I should ever grow tired of it either," Rose murmured.

Three weeks, she thought! And she and Mrs. Wilson-Plunkett had been staying in their hotel for nearly a fortnight now—he had been here on the very night of their arrival, when she had looked up at the crescent moon and wondered in which corner of the world he was at that moment!

He turned to look at her, the faintest of smiles on his face.

"Odd that we should meet again in Rome, of all places, Rose! We say good-bye at Enderby—and come face to face again in the Eternal City!"

His eyes flickered over her very deliberately.

"I like you as you are, Rose, but I shall never forget my small and earnest schoolgirl who sent me such carefully-written letters—and, incidentally, never forgot my birthday!—during the five years that we have known one another! Now come inside and take off that jacket and relax. Would you like some tea? This is a kind of service flat, and I can ring for some."

When the tea arrived and she was sitting in a thin silk blouse with a plain neckline and little collar that drew attention to the girlish column of her throat, he invited her to pour out. Her hair seemed to flame in the pleasant dimness of the room, and although it was beautifully styled, and very carefully looked after, the removal of her hat had ruffled it a little, and that, too, lent her a much younger and less sophisticated look.

"That's better!" the man said as she manipulated the teapot and remembered without asking that he took two lumps of sugar. "I like it when you look less like a fashion-plate. It seems to bring the old Enderby days closer."

"Do you miss them?" Rose asked, longing, but not daring, to ask also whether he was beginning to get over the dreadful disappointment of his frustrated wedding plans. Looking at him, she could hardly tell what he was really feeling like, but she had no doubt at all that his experience had definitely embittered him.

"It's all right, Rose—you can ask me if you want to," he said, smiling into her large eyes as she handed him his cup. The smile twisted his lips a little. "You can ask me anything you like."

"I—I only wanted to know whether—whether you were, perhaps, getting over things a bit . . .?" she managed at last with almost painful shyness.

He absent-mindedly helped himself to another lump of sugar, and watched it drop with a little splash into his tea.

"That sort of thing one either gets over—fairly soon. Or it gets over one—if you can follow me?" looking at her obliquely.

Rose shook her head rather helplessly.

"You mean that it's—the initial shock that's the worst?"

"In my case I think it was—yes!"

"But"—she helped herself to a sugary biscuit and bit into it with a feeling of agitation in her breast—"I should have thought—I mean . . . when one loses someone—one cares for, it's the feeling of loss that grows worse with the—with the passing of time! At least that's how I felt when—when Daddy died . . ."

"Yes, that's what I mean," he agreed gravely. "That is the feeling of acute loss—irreplaceable loss. But there is the loss which is more superficial, and in that case it's the pride that is more badly damaged. And, believe me, damaged pride is a very unpleasant thing to live with for any length of time!"

Rose looked up at him with a feeling of wonder and disbelief. Was he trying to tell her that his love for Heather Willoughby had not been so overwhelming that when she let him down he had not suffered an acute loss—but rather it was the damage to his pride that had worried him?

81

She could understand the horrible laceration to his pride—a man of his years, and in his position, to be treated so shabbily in the eyes of everyone who knew not only him, but the woman who had promised to share his life! Even she felt herself writhing as she thought of the horrible callousness of it, the lack of imagination that made it possible for a woman to do such damage. But he *had* been in love with Heather — it had been the one thing everyone had seemed certain about while the wedding preparations were going forward.

"You see, Rose," Sir Laurence explained—as if he was making the explanation to someone very young and simple, which she actually was—"there are degrees of love, like everything else. There are degrees of hate, fear, resentment—anything you like to mention! And sometimes one doesn't discover until afterwards the particular category into which one's emotion can be placed."

"I see," she said, but he smiled a little because she didn't sound in the least as if she saw at all.

"I don't think you do, my child," he remarked. "Which makes me more than ever certain that you will have to be very careful when the time arrives for you to fall in love yourself! Don't *imagine* yourself in love, and don't get carried away by it! Not," he added, watching her as she bent in some confusion above the teapot and the hot-water jug, "that I believe you ever will imagine yourself in love, Rose. With that hair and the disposition which I feel certain goes with it, you'll probably fall so headlong that it would be fatal for you if anything went wrong."

She didn't dare to glance at him, but he seemed to find her an interesting study for several seconds, and then he got up and walked away to the window.

"So you see, Rose, there was a certain amount of justification for what you said to me that last night at Enderby," he remarked at last, when she had begun to feel that he had forgotten her.

She was silent because she didn't know what to say.

He turned and looked at her.

"Do I disappoint you? I'll confess I was somewhat surprised myself when I made the discovery that I was obviously a person of superficial emotions."

She wanted to reassure him that she didn't think he was—but then there was the evidence of the woman she had seen him with the night before, the rather dazzling Italian woman. Had he already transferred his interest—such interest as he was capable of feeling in any woman—to her? Rose felt a sudden feeling of immense concern rise up in her, and the concern looked out of her eyes, but he was at a loss to understand it.

"If you're more or less—reconciled—to what happened in October, and you miss Enderby very much, why don't you go home again?" she heard herself asking, because she suddenly had to know.

He looked down at the tip of the cigarette he had just lighted, and he seemed to contemplate it thoughtfully before he answered.

"Because at the moment I find Rome attracts me very much—it has something I don't want to say good-bye to yet awhile," he admitted, and Rose felt her heart sink.

The flat bell rang suddenly and sharply, and when he went to open the door Rose heard a woman's voice talking to him in a soft and pleasing Italian voice.

"I do not interrupt anything important?" she asked. "I find you alone, my dear Lance? Yes?"

"No, as a matter of fact I am not alone," Sir Laurence replied as he ushered her into the sitting-room. "Miss Hereward—my ward," looking directly at Rose—"is with me. But you have already met, so there's no need for introductions."

83

Rose had an impression of almost overpowering elegance—the sharp contrast of an immensely smart black suit and white accessories, scarlet lips and brilliant eyes—as Signora Bardoli held out her hand to her. The younger girl stood up, feeling for some reason absurdly self-conscious, and felt the rings hidden by the immaculately gloved fingers biting into her own hands. Signora Bardoli had a cool smile on her lips as she looked her over, and there were few details of Rose's appearance that escaped her.

"How very pleasant we should meet again so soon," the lovely Italian observed in rather an odd voice, her eyes barely smiling. "Can it be that your guardian has been overcome by the thought of his neglect, and is endeavouring to make up for it?"

She looked round, half mockingly, at Sir Laurence, but the expression on his face gave away little.

"Rose and I haven't seen much of one another lately, it's true," he admitted quite briskly, "but she's hardly the type to require a constant eye on her. Are you, Rose?" sending her a faint smile.

"That was not the opinion you held last night," the *signora* reminded him very sweetly. "You were a little concerned to see her receiving so much attention from that handsome young Camillo de Lippi. But perhaps you have discovered that Rose has not lost her heart to him?" with arching delicate brows.

"There is no question of a girl of nineteen losing her heart to—anyone," Sir Laurence returned, rather more brusquely than briskly this time.

His unexpected visitor laughed indulgently.

"Oh, come now, Lance! It is possible to lose one's heart at almost any age, and at nineteen I was already a married woman." She looked at Rose as if there was something about her that amused her. "But in England, of course, your girls do not mature quite so quickly. However, nineteen! . . ." Again her eyebrows ascended, and the arch look in her eyes Rose definitely did not like. "Do not let him bully you, Rose, or coerce you! Love is an experience we can none of us afford to miss."

As Rose, feeling not only embarrassed but as if all the pleasure of the afternoon had vanished from it for her, turned away to pick up her jacket and put it on, she heard the other woman add softly to Sir Laurence:

"As you, my dear Lance, would surely be the last to deny!"

Sir Laurence helped Rose on with her jacket, but he said with a suspicion of a frown between his brows:

"I will take you back to your hotel, Rose, but there is no great hurry. Unless you are in a hurry yourself?"

"Don't attempt to pry into the girl's list of engagements," the *signora* rebuked gaily, but this time his frown was quite noticeable, and she explained quickly that she had only looked in to remind him that the night of the twenty-second was one he must keep absolutely free.

"The Princess de Boccacello is giving a dance for her daughter on that night, and we are both invited. The Princess was insistent that Sir Laurence Melville should receive an invitation," smiling up at him as if she was sure the flattery would please him, which it actually didn't appear to do. "And it is to be a most important dance, with all Rome hoping to be there. Although, of course, there will be many disappointments when invitations are not received."

Sir Laurence said nothing, and Rose pulled on her little hat and picked up her handbag and gloves. Signora Bardoli looked at her in a leisurely, approving manner.

"How charming!" she commented. "You have very good taste, little Rose, for one so young. Or does Mrs. Wilson-Plunkett select your wardrobe for you? You are fortunate in having *two* people so actively interested in you!"

Rose was glad when she was in a taxi, and once more alone with Sir Laurence, driving back to her hotel, but Sir Laurence still appeared to be frowning.

"I intend to see quite a lot of you, Rose," he told her, "while you remain in Rome—and, incidentally, I do, too! And I mean to have that talk with Mrs. Wilson-Plunkett as soon as possible, so don't let her think up any more excuses for avoiding me, will you?"

Rose murmured something non-committal, and thought vaguely that it didn't matter to her very much whether he saw Mrs. Wilson-Plunkett or not. She was no longer any real concern of his, and he had affairs of his own to attend to. Why didn't he attend to them and leave her alone?

She felt strongly, just then, that she would prefer it.

CHAPTER IX

WHEN she got back to the hotel she found that Camillo had been endeavouring to establish contact with her, and the next morning a mass of roses arrived for her from one of Rome's leading florists. They were every colour, from palest pink to creamy yellow, and only one was scarlet as heart's blood. Camillo arrived hard on the heels of his floral tribute, and Rose saw him downstairs in one of the public lounges.

He looked at her reproachfully when she entered, noticing immediately that the scarlet rose was not tucked into the front of her dress as he had half hoped. He was reproachful, too, because he had wanted to take her out to lunch the previous day, but he had been given to understand that she was lunching with the Englishman whom he had met the night before. Rose had not thought it necessary to explain that for five years she had looked upon Sir Laurence as her guardian, and it was plain from Camillo's slightly sullen eyes and injured speech that he resented any encroachments on what he was beginning to look upon as his own particular preserves—whether permanently or not!

Looking at him and thinking, as she always did, that his appearance was almost too romantically perfect for the modern age in which he lived, Rose found herself recalling Sir Laurence's warning against him, and the type he represented. The play-boy type with aristocratic connections, and in fact a lot of noble blood.

Rome, she had discovered, in just over a fortnight, was filled with young men like Camillo, scions of ancient families, not always backed by the generosity of an uncle, but nearly always good-looking in a somewhat spectacular fashion, and the possessors of a great deal of charm.

But she liked to think that Camillo really was charming, that he was sincere and courtly and natural, and not prepared to risk his future happiness in order to secure a rich wife. Without being in the least seriously attracted by him—she was armoured against dangers of that sort in a way Sir Laurence was never likely to guess, or so she sincerely hoped—she did like him very much, and she felt slightly angry with Sir Laurence because, as a result of their conversation yesterday, she might already be beginning to look with doubt upon a very attentive escort. So very attentive, in fact, that it did sometimes worry her.

Camillo was prepared to forgive her for her defection of the day before if she would promise to accompany him to the Princess de Boccacello's dance for her daughter on the night of the twenty-second. Rose was almost touched by this invitation, for out of all the young women he must know in Rome—and had known for a long time—that he should pick on her, a mere tourist, as she looked upon herself, was at least evidence that he liked her very much indeed. And when Mrs. Wilson-Plunkett heard about the invitation she made no attempt to conceal her approval.

"You must have a new dress for the occasion," she said. "Something very special! We will call upon Signor Carmello, who is a very old friend of mine, and see what he can design for you. He will love the opportunity, for not many young women have quite the quality of your looks, Rose."

Rose was often a little embarrassed by Mrs. Wilson-Plunkett's insistence on harping on the quality of her looks, which she herself was too modest to admire very seriously. And in her school days she had considered that red hair was very definitely a handicap, especially when it was allied to definitely greenish eyes.

88

But Signor Carmello, when he saw her, was as enthusiastic as Mrs. Wilson-Plunkett had felt sure he would be. He brought out lengths of material and held them up against her, and in the end he decided that ice-green taffeta with some very light touches of silver embroidery would do much for the exquisite tones of her skin and hair.

The material was draped on her, and young women knelt at her feet with pins, and by the time they departed Signor Carmello was looking thoroughly pleased, and Mrs. Wilson-Plunkett was willing to wager that not even the Princess's daughter would look as attractive as Rose on the night of the dance.

But Rose herself felt oddly depressed, and a little worried—especially when the woman she would persist in regarding as her employer started talking about letting her wear her emerald bracelet and drop ear-rings on the night of the dance. Both the bracelet and the earrings had been recently re-set, and Rose knew their value was far beyond her to replace if she should lose them. In fact she never could replace them. In addition to which this sort of thing could not go on, for she was after all only a stranger to Mrs. Wilson Plunkett, and there was no reason at all why the old lady should behave with such extraordinary generosity towards her.

She often thought she would much prefer it if she really was a companion drawing only a modest weekly wage, or if she could do more to actually repay the amount laid out on her appearance, and present luxurious way of living.

But whenever she hinted at feeling very much under an obligation Mrs. Wilson-Plunkett would smile as if she herself was well content and slightly amused because anyone so young should be conscious of obligation, and assured her more than once:

"Don't worry, my dear. One of these days I shall be well repaid! I feel it in my bones that one day I shall be very proud of you," and Rose's anxiety was not lessened but increased by this prophecy concerning her future.

Returning from Signor Carmello's elegant modern *salon* in one of Rome's most modern quarters, the girl was actually feeling as if she was overhung by a shadow, and the shadow only partly lifted when she discovered that Sir Laurence was waiting for them in their hotel. Sir Laurence looked as if he had been waiting very determinedly for the moment when the heavy plate-glass doors yielded to their entrance, and Mrs. Wilson-Plunkett, when she saw him rise up from one of the deep, comfortable chairs in the shadow of a solid bank of exotic hothouse flowers, looked almost as determined that she was not going to be waylaid in this fashion.

"This is not an hour of the day when I am at my best, Sir Laurence," she said a little tartly, although her bright eyes regarded him with just a hint of approval because of his extremly masculine and very personable appearance. "However, if you care to drink an aperitif with us I can spare you ten minutes or so before going up to dress."

"I would like to have ten minutes with you alone, Mrs. Wilson-Plunkett, if you don't mind," Sir Laurence returned—a trifle grimly, Rose thought, and then noticed that he looked at her rather pointedly.

Mrs. Wilson-Plunkett smiled with unusual acidity.

"You can take a hint as well as anyone else, I expect Rose?" she said. "Go upstairs and enjoy a leisurely bath while I talk to your former guardian."

The way she deliberately accented the words "former guardian" did not cause Sir Laurence to look any less grim; but before Rose took her departure he stopped her with a gesture.

"Just a minute, Rose! I was wondering whether you would have dinner with me tonight—if Mrs. Wilson-Plunkett has no objection?" very dryly.

There was silence for several seconds, and then the old lady shrugged her shoulders.

"It's up to Rose," she declared. "I am not her keeper."

Rose felt all her pulses give an absurd little leap, and then the beat of her heart slowed as she remembered Signora Bardoli. Was this a night when he could not see her, and therefore was somewhat at a loose end? And being at a loose end, was that why he wanted her to dine with him?

She looked at Mrs. Wilson-Plunkett as if for guidance and a general directive, but her employer shook her head with a faint smile.

"You must make up your own mind, Rose!"

So Rose coloured faintly and said that she would be very pleased to accept the invitation, and Sir Laurence said he would call for her in about a couple of hours. And when she had finally left them and was on her way up to her room in the lift, he looked round at the somewhat smug-faced elderly lady who had just given an order to an extremely obsequious waiter, and remarked:

"So you're not really trying to influence her against me?"

"My dear Sir Laurence," Mrs. Wilson-Plunkett returned with the tartness to which she was addicted at times, "I have already told you that I am not Rose's keeper, but I don't mind letting you know that I have plans for her! If you chose, when your wedding arrangements became unstuck, to disappear into the blue and leave her to the care of your housekeeper at Enderby, and with no other more detailed plans made for her, you can hardly blame me if she decided that she preferred to be free of your guardianship! And in any case it's absurd that a man of your age should be guardian to a young woman of her age—an extraordinarily beautiful and very charming young woman at that!"

"I quite agree," Sir Laurence returned with an imperturbable expression. "And that's why I have formed another plan for Rose's future! Do you care to listen to me while I outline it?"

Looking back upon the dinner that night with Sir Laurence in the quiet of her room afterwards, Rose decided it was one of the pleasantest evenings that had ever happened to her in the whole of her lifetime.

There was nothing formal about the evening, nothing strained, or embarrassing either. Sir Laurence took her to a rather small but very exclusive restaurant where they dined quietly and extremely well without an orchestra to entertain them, or a dance floor to tempt them, and for the first time since he abruptly made up his mind to marry Heather Willoughby, and Rose received her first intimation of his intentions, they talked together naturally as in the old days, and on the topics that had been wont to appeal to them both.

Enderby and the various improvements that could still be made to it, Thatcher and his determination never to depart from the formality of the perfect manservant. They also talked about Sir Laurence's own plans for his immediate future—that is to say, his business plans and the new architectural designs he was working on and becoming engrossed in. He was particularly interested in designs for a new modern cathedral he had been invited to submit, and deriving a good deal of inspiration from his visits to Roman churches, both Renaissance and the more austere styles of the Counter-Reformation period. The

Baroque churches with the lively façades did not appeal to him so much.

Then he had plans for a new ultra-modern hospital, and a block of flats. As she looked across the table at him and saw the genuine enthusiasm that was written in his face, and how magically it seemed almost to banish the haggard lines she had so particularly noticed a few days ago, Rose knew a sensation of sudden happiness for his sake, because there were things that could still interest him acutely.

"You're a wonderful listener, Rose," he told her when he saw how her eyes watched him, and realized that she was really listening attentively and not with anything forced about her marked air of interest, even absorption in what he was saying. "You always were. You were one of the few schoolgirls who never chattered."

Rose smiled faintly.

"I expect I did all my chattering at school."

"I decline to believe it." He smiled back at her, thinking how well her little black cocktail dress suited her—in fact almost anything suited her. "You're one of the people who like to take things in, and that makes you restful. Reposeful is perhaps a better word. You're gentle and feminine, too—very feminine." His eyes continued to rest on her. "I don't think you realize how lovely you are, Rose. No wonder Heather didn't like you!"

And then he abruptly changed the subject, and shortly after that they decided to walk part of the way home because it was such a perfect night. Their footsteps echoed as they strolled along, although there were plenty of people strolling on all sides of them, and in the quieter thoroughfares they sometimes caught a snatch of dance music or an accordion being played somewhere behind discreetly veiled windows.

And above them huge stars hung in the velvety

sable sky, and a moon at its full climbed above the sluggishly flowing Tiber and the misty Alban hills. Sleek cars rolled past, and feminine perfumes floated on the wind—feminine and fresh flower perfumes from the night-enshrouded gardens of Rome.

Rose felt Sir Laurence's hand lightly grasping her elbow, and as he guided and directed her steps she thought:

The Eternal City! . . . The city to which one would return if one dropped a coin in the Fountain de Trevi! And she had dropped a coin in the fountain, and she had wished, too, and part of her wish had come true.

She had wished that Sir Laurence, who had disappeared out of her life, might reappear again, even if it was only for a short time. And here he was beside her, sharing with her the magic of the Roman night!

CHAPTER X

THE night of the dance arrived at last. Rose's dress had been safely delivered from Signor Camillo, and there was no doubt about it, it was a dream of a dress.

Mrs. Wilson-Plunkett looked so satisfied when Rose put it on that the girl would not have been surprised to hear her start purring like a contented cat. She looked like a contented cat with her head on one side, making vague noises which signified approval, and it was only when she went to her jewel-case and extracted the recently re-set emerald bracelet and matching ear-rings that Rose ceased to feel amused.

But Mrs. Wilson-Plunkett was nothing if not obstinate, and she fastened the bracelet on Rose's wrist, and then held up one of the ear-rings against a creamy pale ear. But the effect was too sophisticated, and she removed it at once, deciding that the bracelet was sufficient adornment.

"Sir Laurence will not approve," she remarked as she made certain that the safety-catch of the bracelet was secured. "But it doesn't matter whether he approves or not. He has his plans for you, and I have mine!"

And then she stepped back in order to admire Rose afresh, but the girl was looking vaguely concerned by her remarks. She had no intention of allowing anyone to make plans for her future, but until she knew what those plans were she could do or say nothing about them.

The old lady clucked afresh, as if she was entirely responsible for the way the girl looked. And certainly the touch of silver on the tiny close-fitting bodice of the ice-green taffeta seemed to put stars into Rose's eyes. The lines of the dress were flowing and graceful, enhancing Rose's youthful dignity, and although it left her camellia-pale shoulders completely bare there was a stole that went with it that was also delicately touched with silver embroidery.

Her hair had never looked better, but she was a little pale for a gala occasion, Mrs. Wilson-Plunkett thought. And yet she approved the pallor. It made her look like an ice-maiden—ice and fire with that hair!

Yes, Signor Camillo had done very well, the rich widow thought, watching the fire that also streaked from the bracelet on the girl's slender wrist.

When Camillo arrived for Rose he looked almost taken aback by her appearance. Mrs. Wilson-Plunkett studied his reaction with sensations of mounting satisfaction. He had wanted to send flowers for Rose to wear, but the older woman had said no. No flowers for Rose with that dress. She was perfect as she was. And Camillo, escorting her out to the ivory and black car, was in complete agreement.

When they arrived at the Princess de Boccacello's *Palazzo*, where every one of the vast rooms seemed to be filled with guests, almost the first person Rose received a whole-hearted compliment from on her appearance was Prince Paul de Lippi. Looking so distinguished in full evening dress that for an instant Rose found it difficult to conceal from him her admiration for the way he looked, he bent over her hand and kissed it, as his nephew had once done on another occasion. His eyes, deeper and darker than Camillo's, gentler but just as filled with admiration, looked into hers.

"You are so lovely that you quite take my breath away!" he said. "Although I can't compete with Camillo as a dancing partner, may I dance with you later on?"

"Of course," Rose answered shyly, and she thought that Camillo drew her away rather quickly, and had the impression that the Prince stood looking after them as they disappeared into the press.

Camillo presented her to her hostess, but Francesca, for whom the dance was being given, was too surrounded by admirers and special friends for anyone who had arrived late, as they had, to get near to her. But about half-way through the evening Rose had a chance to observe her very closely, and she was a little surprised by what she saw. Someone rather small and fragile and obviously young—perhaps barely seventeen— with enormous dark eyes and a faint, rather hectic colour in her cheeks, dressed all in white, who, when she first caught sight of Camillo, seemed actually to look at him a little reproachfully. And Camillo, Rose felt somehow certain, was not entirely at his ease as he gave vent to a string of rather fulsome flatteries and bent over her hand, in the same way that his uncle had recently bent over Rose's, and introduced the English girl.

Rose felt the strange, luminous and penetrating eyes of Francesa remained glued to her face for several seconds, and at the end of her inspection the small scarlet mouth seemed to become pursed a little, and once again Camillo received a very long and deliberate look. Rose even felt a little embarrassed as she stood there, and she was glad when a young man swooped upon Francesca, the orchestra that was ensconced behind a solid bank of white roses started to play after a brief pause an old-fashioned Viennese waltz, and Camillo swept her, too, back on to the dance floor.

As she looked up at him she thought that his face looked frowning and disturbed, but he smiled at her suddenly as he felt her eyes upon him— recognizing that frown and that look of disturbance—and drew her suddenly closely to him.

97

"You are lovelier far than anyone else here to-night," he told her. "We will forget everything but that, shall we?"

But this time it was Rose who frowned, and when later she caught him looking at the emerald bracelet on her wrist and heard him express admiration for it, a definite twinge of uneasiness stabbed at her. She remembered what Sir Laurence had said about handsome young Romans attached to noble families.

She knew nothing about the Boccacello family, but from the magnificence of this dance tonight they were wealthy enough. But one could never be sure about a thing like that, and it was always unwise to judge from appearances. The Princess de Boccacello was a widow, and she had more than one daughter to marry off.

Later Rose found she was called upon to keep her promise to Prince Paul, and in spite of the fact that he had denied being a very good dancer, she discovered that he actually was a very good dancer indeed. She had been looking everywhere for some sign of Sir Laurence and the Signora Bardoli, but although she had understood that they were putting in an appearance, having, as she knew, both received invitations, she saw nothing at all of them for an hour and more after her own arrival. Camillo had been forced temporarily to abandon her, and dance with someone else, and she was standing for the first time that evening alone when the Prince came up behind her.

"I think I can manage this," he said, smiling, and guided her through the movements of a rumba. As she had not so far observed him dancing with anyone else that evening—although he had talked to quite a few of the dowagers who formed the usual groups—she was not altogether surprised to find that eyes followed their progress with a certain amount of barely-concealed interest, and when, as soon as the dance was over, Prince Paul took her arm and suggested that they seek a breath of fresh air outside she had the feeling that the interest quickened a little.

It was a breathlessly beautiful Roman night, and the gardens of the *Palazzo* were a paradise to wander in after the heat and the close pressure of humanity inside. Rose recalled the night when she had dined at the de Lippi villa, and her host had shown her his garden himself, and on that occasion she had thought him delightful. Tonight, with one of his slender patrician hands under her elbow, he guided her along the paths, and when they came to a little pavilion, like a toy pavilion of marble, he suggested that they sat down for a while in a couple of comfortable chairs placed inside.

"That is if you are warm enough," he said, and gently touched her bare shoulder where the stole had slipped.

If Camillo had touched her shoulder in the same way she would have been inclined to shrink away and resent his touch a little, in spite of the fact that she found him generally charming; but with the Prince she felt perfectly able to relax, and accepted a cigarette, and even allowed him to pull the stole up about her shoulders a little when a flower-laden breeze reached them inside the pavilion.

But when the breeze died away it was very still, and very pleasant, with the flower perfume delicate and yet penetrating, hanging in the atmosphere like a silken caress. And in front of them was the star-pricked panorama of Rome, too vague to be anything but a blur, but with a flash of moonlight catching the twists of the Tiber, and the sudden thrust of a triumphal arch.

The Prince enabled her after a time to distinguish the huge masses of the walls of the Palatine and the Forum, and finally the Colosseum. But she liked to think that side by side with these

99

indestructible giants and the grimness they exuded, there were the more gracious buildings of Rome and a warm and attractive way of life.

"I wonder how you like it here?" the Prince asked her softly at last. "Have you thrown a coin into the Fountain de Trevi?"

"Oh, yes," she answered, smiling at him.

"So you will come back!" he exclaimed. "And you wish to come back?"

"Of course. As a matter of fact," she confessed, clasping her hands about her slim knees and leaning a little forward to peer out across that terra-cotta bowl which held Rome like a giant hand, "I can think of nothing more pleasant than to spend the whole of one's life here."

"But you would miss your own country," he assured her. "You would wish to go back."

"I don't know." Suddenly her voice sounded flat and a little wistful. For where was there in England, unless she went on accepting the benevolent charity of Mrs. Wilson-Plunkett and made her London flat her home, that which she could call her rightful place of residence? Certainly not Enderby, where so much of her so often longed to be! Enderby, where she had always felt curiously safe and secure, but where all her happy memories had been smirched by that final night. "I don't know," she repeated, and sighed.

The Prince leaned forward also to peer at her gently.

"You and Mrs. Wilson-Plunkett are not related?" he asked.

Rose shook her head.

"No. I suppose you could say that she is my employer, but she is far too generous to be an ordinary employer."

"She appears to be very fond of you," he said. His eyes dropped to the emerald bracelet sparkling on her wrist. "Perhaps she thinks of you in the light of a daughter."

Rose looked worried. Her eyes, too, dropped to the emerald bracelet, and she realized how it helped to camouflage the truth about her. That she was an impecunious nobody, and had no right at all to be dressed up like this, in spite of her expensive education, and the advantages it had equipped her with. And suddenly she decided to tell him the truth, not mentioning Sir Laurence by name, but giving him plainly to understand that, such as she was, she was the product of acts of generosity on the part first of a guardian who had had no need to be her guardian, and then Mrs. Wilson-Plunkett, who was more or less actuated by a whim.

"This dress," she said, touching the expensive, specially designed ice-blue gown, "cost more than I could reasonably expect to earn in a good many weeks. And the rest of my wardrobe cost a great deal more. Sometimes it worries me."

"Poor little Rose!" he exclaimed softly, and she turned towards him as if she was suddenly startled, for the only man who had ever called her "Poor little Rose" in quite that tone was Sir Laurence, and somehow the utterance disturbed her. "Poor little Rose," the Prince repeated. "Why have you told me all this?"

Rose looked down at the bracelet again and resented its sparkling green fire.

"Because I thought you ought to know. Because I—because I was afraid I might be creating the wrong kind of impression."

"So far as I am concerned," he told her, and his voice was more gentle even than a caress, "the impression you have already created is not likely to be affected by any revelations you care to make to me about yourself. It is—an ineradicable impression!" He paused for a moment, looking at her in the dim light. "But if you're thinking of my nephew Camillo—well, I do not think that your very private affairs are any concern of his, and it is possible that your Mrs. Wilson-Plunkett would prefer that the world should draw its own conclusions about the two of you, and the relationship in which you stand to one another. Don't you agree with me?"

"You mean," Rose said a little falteringly, "that I really hadn't any right to tell—even you . . .?"

"Not at all," he returned in that gentle voice of his. "And as a matter of fact there was no need to tell me. Mrs. Wilson-Plunkett has already told me quite a lot about you," smiling at her and lightly patting one of her hands.

Rose's delicate brows crinkled.

"But why should she bother to talk to you about—me?"

"Why should she not talk about you?" His eyes appraised her, twinkling a little as if something about her amused him. "You are too modest, Rose, and not nearly as shrewd as your Mrs. Wilson-Plunkett. And, of course, she wouldn't have discussed you with me if she hadn't gathered that I was—interested!"

Rose's eyes grew large and a trifle wondering as she gazed at him, but his expression did not alter, and suddenly he suggested that they ought to return to the others.

"I mustn't be selfish and keep you here," he said. "But"—and again his hand touched hers—"whatever your present background, Rose, there is a great deal of security waiting for you if—and whenever!—you feel inclined to seize hold of it! Perhaps you will think about that sometimes!"

And Rose returned to the house full of lights and music with the bewildered conviction taking root in her mind that what he intended to convey was not what her slightly stunned feminine intuition was more or less certain he intended to convey.

When they returned to the house almost the first two people she saw dancing together were Signora Bardoli and Sir Laurence Melville. Sir Laurence, looking at his best in white tie and tails, would have been easily recognizable to her at a far greater distance than that which separated them, and Signora Bardoli was wearing a brilliant scarlet confection that would have made it impossible for her to be passed over by anyone.

The music was just ending when they entered, and Sir Laurence and his partner moved towards Rose as the Prince bent almost tenderly over her hand and told her that he was just about to take his departure.

"But I shall see you again—soon, I hope," he said, and looked for a moment with definite meaning into her eyes. Then he disappeared as Sir Laurence reached the side of his erstwhile ward.

"You should feel flattered, Miss Hereward," Signora Bardoli declared, "because the Prince pays you such marked attention! It's already a subject for gossip that he actually danced with you, and then you disappear together into the gardens of the *Palazzo!*" Her amused eyes swept upwards to Lance's face. "Your little ward is a credit to you, Lance," she told him. "You must have trained her very well, and probably the rewards will be richer than you thought!"

But Sir Laurence didn't appear to share her amusement, and in fact there was almost a stern look of disapproval on his face as his eyes fixed themselves upon Rose's face.

"I understood you were coming here with that young man Camillo," he said with quite noticeable coldness. "Or did I make a mistake and was it the uncle?"

"Oh, come now!" Lola Bardoli interposed, still looking amused. "The uncle has the money, and they both have looks, and Rose would be a simpleton if she couldn't decide which she liked best out

103

of the two! And if I were in her place I know which of the two I would convince myself that I ought to like best. But perhaps I'm a little too worldly," noticing Rose's withdrawn look of distaste.

"If Rose is worldly at nineteen I shudder to think what she'll be like at twenty-nine!" Sir Laurence exclaimed very shortly.

"Very charming," the *signora* assured him smoothly. *"Completely* charming, I would say, especially to the man of discernment! And to-night she is looking delightful in that dress. Was it Carmello, my dear?" she inquired of Rose.

The latter nodded.

"I thought I was not mistaken," Signora Bardoli murmured. "Your Mrs. Wilson-Plunkett has the right ideas about you, I can see. She is, as you would say in England, putting her money on the right horse!"

But Rose, feeling a strong sensation of revulsion at being thus inspected by her, and not missing the way in which she clung possessively to Sir Laurence's arm, was glad to see Camillo threading his way towards them through the throng. Camillo was not looking very much happier than he had looked earlier in the evening, but at least she thought he could remove her from the necessity of attempting conversation with anyone quite like the *signora*.

But before Camillo, after looking almost defiantly at Sir Laurence, whisked her away, the latter inquired with cool, clear earnestness:

"Enjoying yourself, Rose?"

"Yes." She turned to smile at him with assumed brilliance. "It's a wonderful evening!"

But not, she thought a little sickly, as Camillo led her away, as wonderful as the evening when she had walked the streets of Rome at his side!

"What a question to ask anyone of her age," Signora Bardoli remarked as Sir Laurence stood watching Rose's slender retreating figure with an odd look in his eyes. "Of course it's a wonderful evening for her. And if you're thinking of asking her to dance later on I wouldn't. You mustn't be a spoil-sport, you know!" tapping him gently on the arm with her gold-mesh evening bag. "And there can't be much glamour about a man who has once stood in the relationship of a guardian to one, even if for some reason the guardianship seems to have ended!"

Sir Laurence's eyes narrowed, and he looked down at her rather sharply.

"You really think that?" he asked.

She shrugged slightly.

"Well, darling"—the way she said "darling" was rather attractive in her soft Italian voice— "what do you think yourself?" Her amused eyes went to his temples, where the few silvery hairs showed up against the sleek, well-disciplined brownness that made his head look very polished and groomed. "If you were still only nineteen, wouldn't the middle thirties strike you as a little—remote?"

So Rose was not provided with the opportunity to dance once with the man on whom her thoughts dwelt so constantly throughout the whole evening, but she observed that he danced a good deal with Lola Bardoli. And when the evening ended and Camillo took her back to her hotel, she was not in a mood to respond to his sudden desire to pay her a great deal of attention.

It was really very late—or, rather, extremely early in the morning—and there was absolutely no one about as they left the car and walked through the little enclosed courtyard before the hotel to the impressive entrance. The shadows fell thickly across the paved walks and flower borders, with an inevitable fountain playing in the centre of what in daylight was a positive feast of colour, and in one of the blackest of the shadows Camillo suddenly paused. Rose paused also, and looked up at her escort.

In an instant she was in his arms, and she could feel his mouth pressing hotly and ardently against the remote coolness of her own lips—hitherto quite untouched by masculine ones. For an instant, so surprised was she, that she actually submitted to this quite unexpected act of love-making on his part, and he kissed her with a violence that seemed actually to scorch her mouth.

And then she drew away determinedly.

"Oh, Rose," Camillo whispered, looking down at her in the faint light, "it would be so easy to fall in love with you! So very easy!"

But Rose had already made up her mind that night that if he was in love with anyone it was Princess de Boccacello's seventeen-year-old daughter Francesca. And while admitting the power of her own feminine attraction at that late hour after a highly successful dance in which they had danced a great deal together, she suddenly felt rather acutely disappointed in him. Sir Laurence was right, she thought heavily, feeling the weight of the emerald bracelet on her wrist. And the fact that Camillo admitted that it *would* be easy to fall in love with her—not that he *had* fallen in love with her!—allowed her to see quite plainly what he was endeavouring to force himself to do.

And she thought, with a touch of wistfulness this time, what a pity men—nice men like Camillo, who were so full of a very real charm, should be prepared to overlook the important things in life like that. What a pity Sir Laurence, who had just escaped a marriage which might well have turned out to be quite disastrous, should be acknowledging the charm of yet another woman who was—Rose felt absolutely certain—not the right type of woman for him!

But when she was undressing in her hotel bedroom she looked at herself in her dressing-table mirror and thought how violently her lips flamed. She touched them as if the sight of them vaguely excited and disturbed her—or was it the remembrance of Camillo's ardent kisses?

It was impossible, apparently, to receive kisses even from a man in whom one was not particularly interested without having them upset one in a curious way. It was just as if a lid had been lifted, and all sorts of unguessed emotions and longing rose up and clamoured for attention.

She felt unpleasantly shaken as she went on with her undressing, trying not to imagine what it would be like if another man's arms had caught at her and held her fiercely out there under the last light of the stars, and another man's lips come close to hers . . .

CHAPTER XI

Two days later she again saw Signora Bardoli, only this time the *signora* was without an escort, and had in fact just emerged from beneath a hair-drier in the same exclusive establishment devoted to increasing feminine appeal where Rose herself had been having her hair washed and set. The two met when Rose was paying her bill, and the exquisite young woman behind the counter was booking her an appointment for the following week. Signora Bardoli stepped out of her cubicle and literally beamed at Rose.

"Ah!" she exclaimed. "It is the little English Rose! We meet when we can have an opportunity for talk, unless you are in a great hurry?"

Rose admitted that she was not in any particular hurry, for Mrs. Wilson-Plunkett was spending the day with an old friend who had just arrived in Rome. She had, as a matter of fact, been wondering what she would do with herself for the rest of the day, and was planning to visit her favourite fountain and try and make up her mind when the *signora* suggested having coffee together.

"We will get my chauffeur to drop us in the Via Veneto," she said. "Those little pavement cafés are rather amusing, and one sees so much that is going on around one."

Rose agreed, and outside the hairdresser's Lola Bardoli's beautifully sleek car waited for her, with a chauffeur and a poodle already occupying it, and in the Via Veneto the car was dismissed, although not the poodle, which its owner took affectionately under her arm.

Rose found it a little difficult to decide upon the exact status the Signorina Bardoli occupied in Roman society. She was obviously a very wealthy widow—if she was a widow—and she dressed superbly. She had excellent taste, and a certain amount of culture, striking looks which she tended so carefully that it was wellnigh impossible to guess her age—although she *could* be anything between thirty and forty, Rose thought. Perhaps even older.

And although she dressed so well and had a small fortune in diamonds on her fingers, and about her statuesque throat and in her small, perfect ears, there was a certain harshness about her which suggested she had not always been used to affluence. A hardness which indicated that she had had to fight for what she had obtained. There was a cynicism, too, in her looks, and particularly in the cool, amused smile which so often stole into her eyes.

Today she looked at Rose and very deliberately took in every detail of her appearance, and complimented her on her hair style which was new and attractive.

"That slightly wind-blown effect suits you," she said while they sipped their coffee, and a slight breeze did its best to make the ruffled effect a little more noticeably ruffled. "You have the youth, and the small, heart-shaped face which it enhances. And that pale primrose suit is most becoming."

It was—and once again the general effect was that of ice and fire—the refreshing coolness of a lemon ice against the rich warmth of Titian hair.

"Tell me about yourself," Signora Bardoli requested suddenly. "Lance is very vague about you, you know"—a slight smile touched her lips—"at one time I thought deliberately vague. I'm afraid I didn't quite believe in his story of a ward."

Rose's eyes widened so much, and were so clear and translucent and faintly shocked that the older woman looked away.

"You didn't?"

"No, my dear. I have met men before who have produced—wards!"

"But I've known Lance—Sir Laurence—ever since I was fourteen! And my father knew him for years before that!"

"Quite." Lola produced a delicate toy of a platinum cigarette-case from her handbag and snapped it open. She passed it across the table to Rose, but the girl shook her head. "I believe everything I'm expected to believe of you now, including Sir Laurence's own testimonial to the unsullied freshness and charm of your character. I even accept that he has a kind of fatherly affection for you, looking upon you as very young and vulnerable and as someone he is anxious to protect from the snares and delusions of this wicked world!" with a kind of derisive sparkle lighting up her eyes. "The only thing I am not quite certain about," allowing the poodle to put his well-manicured paws on her chest and nibble gently at her beautifully made-up cheek, "is what exactly *you* feel for *him*!"

Rose felt her face flame instantly in a most revealing fashion, and the *signora* laughed softly, whilst at the same time restraining the poodle.

"Young girls of your age are not like men of Sir Laurence's age. They do form violent attachments for men older than themselves. But," as if it was part of her duty to reassure, "they do get over them!"

Rose took a hasty gulp at her coffee, and felt as if she actually blushed all over. She wished ardently in that moment that she had not encountered this elegant and—she felt—deliberately taunting Italian woman at the hairdressers, and she was appalled because she was obviously so very transparent. Perhaps even Sir Laurence himself knew!

"No, my dear," Lola told her, just a touch of commiseration as well as the bright gleam of humour in her velvety eyes, "you don't really give away all the secrets of your heart to the world at large, but I happen to be rather perceptive."

Rose said nothing—feeling there was nothing she could say just then—and the *signora* ordered more coffee. When the waiter had accepted the order and departed she repeated:

"But, as I said, you *will* get over it, so don't worry! At nineteen these affairs, especially when they're one-sided, are painful, but they don't last. And in your case you have a couple of very attractive admirers to help you forget, so the cure should be fairly rapid."

Rose found her voice at last.

"I don't think I understand what you are talking about," she managed.

"Don't you?" Lola flashed her a faintly contemptuous glance. "Well, it doesn't really matter, because there are other things I would like to discuss with you—something I would like you to tell me. Sir Laurence's broken engagement—the unhappy ending to his marriage plans! Was the young woman in question very attractive?"

"I—"And then Rose broke off, the breath literally catching in her throat as she stared into a passing taxi. It couldn't be—no; it would be too much like "talking of the devil" to be really true, and in any case she knew she was making a mistake—but for one moment she had thought she recognized a face. It was a lovely face, framed in a cloud of golden hair, and with an absurd little hat mounted on top of it. There had even been a familiar, faintly peevish expression on the face.

"Is anything wrong?" Signora Bardoli demanded.

"No—no, I—I thought I recognized someone . . ."

"But it was a mistake?"

"Yes."

The *signora* sank back and looked a little impatient.

"The young woman Sir Laurence so very nearly married—did you know her?"

"I was to be her bridesmaid."

"You were?" An amazed look, followed by a look of open amusement, made Rose long to escape. "But, my poor dear child—how dreadful!" And then, with silvery laughter in the voice: "But how slow you were! Have you never heard of catching a man on the rebound? Why, Rose, you missed the chance of a lifetime! If Sir Laurence is the man you imagine yourself in love with you could, with your looks and a little cleverness, have got him to turn to you for sympathy if nothing else! And sympathy can lead quite a long way if you're very determined."

This time Rose stood up.

"I think I must be getting back," she said stiffly. "Mrs. Wilson-Plunkett—"

But the *signora* waved her back into her seat.

"I won't keep you longer than another few minutes," she promised. "And I'm sorry if I've upset your sensitive feelings. However, I do think you were rather foolish, Rose. A man when he's been badly hurt really does need sympathy, and you were on the spot to administer it. Because you didn't do so he came to Italy, and I was able to do what I could. For, of course, he told me the whole sorry story, and of course, I could not have been *more* sympathetic! One does feel sympathy readily when a man is as attractive as Sir Laurence. But that any woman should have been foolish enough to let him go . . ." She shook her sleekly coiffured head as if she was genuinely amazed. "It is beyond my comprehension to understand it."

It was beyond Rose's, but she could not say so. She also wondered what the Italian woman would say if she confessed that instead of sympathizing with Sir Laurence she had accused him of stupidity. She, who had no right to accuse him of anything!

"But I feel great curiosity about this—this extraordinary fellow-countryman of yours who did not apparently understand all that she was letting go! Was the man she ran off with unusually attractive?"

Rose tried to recall him.

"No," she admitted, "I don't think that he was."

"Had he, then, a better position than Sir Laurence?"

"No, definitely not!"

"So?" The sleek eyebrows lifted. "It was, perhaps, the result of a quarrel?"

"I—I don't know . . ." But Rose felt suddenly a little cold and sick inside, recalling the accusation Sir Laurence, in his bitterness and anger, had hurled at her.

The *signora* consulted her wristlet watch.

"I must go," she said. "I have a luncheon engagement. But before we part, please tell me this . . . Do you think that Sir Laurence has got over it?"

Rose stood helplessly in front of her.

"I couldn't possibly hazard an opinion."

"No?" The dark eyes now definitely mocked her. "But the eyes of love are perceptive, and I'm sure you have a fairly shrewd idea that he is over it just a little, shall we say? Perhaps he has even recovered altogether!"

Rose was wandering a little aimlessly in the sunshine, and trying to thrust the recent conversation right out of her mind, when a black car stopped near the edge of the kerb, and she looked up to see Sir Laurence seated behind the wheel of his own Bentley and smiling at her.

"Get in Rose." He held open the door for her quickly, and as she subsided on to the seat beside him he returned to the stream of traffic. "You were looking very serious," he told her, "in fact very sober." He glanced at her rather searchingly sideways. "Is everything all right?"

113

"Yes, of course."

Suddenly his hand covered one of hers and pressed it for an instant.

"There's no 'of course' about it! You have a perfect right to look sometimes as if you really are grown up, and Life has already started to hurl a few of its perplexities at you—which it will do with increasing regularity as you grow still older! But so long as you weren't worrying about that young man Camillo, as a result of some defection on his part, I don't mind."

"I wasn't even thinking about Camillo," she assured him.

"Well, that's something I can feel heartily thankful for, because, as you may have gathered, I don't approve of him—or his type!" He turned off into a quieter thoroughfare. "Where do you want me to drop you, Rose? Are you going back to the hotel for lunch, or are you free?"

She confessed to him that she was free as air until evening—and then wondered whether that sounded as if she was angling for an invitation to have lunch with him—and he exclaimed with obvious pleasure:

"Then that's splendid! You can spend the rest of the day with me! I've just had my car sent over from England, and I feel as if I want to use it. But unless you'd prefer to go somewhere very smart for lunch we could have it at my flat. We can talk more comfortably there, and, as I explained, it's a service flat. What do you say?"

"Oh, yes," she answered at once, "I think that would be very nice."

"Really?"

"Yes, honestly."

Once again he patted her hand.

"You're such a nice child, Rose, and a very simple one at heart! I don't think high life appeals to you all that much. I think you were just as happy at Enderby as having your hand saluted by one of the most eligible widowers in Rome. Or is Mrs. Wilson-Plunkett right, and am I wrong?"

Rose puckered her brows.

"I don't quite know what you mean."

"Don't you? Well, never mind—" stealing a very gentle and mildly caressing sideways glance at her this time. "We won't spoil our day by discussing subjects of that sort. Instead, tell me what you think Enderby is looking like now."

Rose sighed without quite realizing that she did so.

"I think it's looking absolutely heavenly, as it always does in the spring. There will be bluebells in the woods, and the wallflowers will be just dying off under the south terrace. The aubretia will be at its best in those large urns that decorate the terrace, and in the drive the rhododendrons and the azaleas will be like a solid wall of colour. There will be every shade, from palest pink to creamy yellow, and the scent—the scent will be the sort of scent that gets up into your head, like honeysuckle in high summer!"

Sir Laurence forgot to concentrate on the traffic and the road ahead for an instant as he glanced at her this time in pure amazement.

"Why, Rose," he exclaimed, "you've painted quite a picture! Does Enderby mean as much to you as all that?"

She nodded her head soberly.

"All that and more. I shall never forget Enderby!"

When they arrived at his flat he escorted her up in the lift, and his eyes looked rather thoughtful as they rested on her face. It was slightly flushed with the excitement of meeting him, and her eyes had that strange look of luminosity about them which not only added to their brilliance, but lent depth to their colour. And the long dark eyelashes wavered above them shyly.

"Perhaps I'm being a little unconventional in bringing you here, Rose," he remarked with an odd twist to his lips when they entered his sitting-room. "I'm inclined to forget that you're no longer a schoolgirl, and that you no longer regard me as a guardian. Mrs. Wilson-Plunkett wouldn't thank me for compromising you at this highly promising stage of your career."

Rose didn't know how to reply to this, and he telephoned for lunch to be brought up to them, and then went to her and took her by her slender shoulders.

"Do you fancy the idea of being Princess Paul de Lippi, Rose?"

Rose's colour deepened uncontrollably, but she also looked considerably taken aback.

"Why do you ask me that?"

"Because that is Mrs. Wilson-Plunkett's plan for you! Camillo she has, of course, never entertained seriously as a suitor for you, although she permits him to take you about. But the Prince—the Prince she thinks about very seriously!"

"I don't think I like this sort of conversation," Rose declared, twisting away from him rather suddenly and looking all at once a little aloof. "I don't think it's very nice, somehow."

He smiled at her gently.

"But that *is* Mrs. Wilson-Plunkett's plan for you and even if she isn't entirely confident of bringing it off, she's certainly got high hopes. You were the talk of the dance the other night, Rose—the little English girl with red hair, whose dress was not quite like any other young woman's dress! The enchanting little English girl!"

"Anyone could look enchanting dressed up like that," Rose insisted, and Sir Laurence's smile grew warmer.

"Well, I'm glad you haven't really changed, Rose," he told her.

The arrival of their meal put an end to that sort of conversation for the time being, but afterwards, on the balcony, sipping their coffee and companionably smoking cigarettes, the man made an attempt to return to it.

"What were you doing this morning, Rose, when I met you?" he asked. "And with whom had you just parted company? You don't normally drift about Rome by yourself, do you?"

"No," Rose admitted, "although I quite enjoy being by myself sometimes, and my favourite occupation is looking at the fountains. I think they're breath-takingly lovely—all of them!"

"You've thrown a coin into the Fountain de Trevi, of course?"

"Oh, yes."

"Did you wish? Tell me what you wished, Rose?"

"It wouldn't come true if I did tell you," looking at him suddenly rather solemnly. And then the sudden remembrance that part of her wish had already come true caused her to blush faintly.

"This is interesting," Sir Laurence remarked, studying her. "You won't tell me what you wished for, but it actually causes you to blush a little. Was it something very nice, Rose?"

But Rose declined to be baited by him, and tossed back her head with a graceful gesture. Suddenly she succeeded in shattering a certain amount of his complaisance.

"I had coffee with *Signora* Bardoli this morning," she told him.

"Oh!" He looked almost taken aback. "Did she ask you to have coffee with her?"

"Yes. We met at the hairdresser's."

"And what did the pair of you talk about?" a litle dryly, while he calmly selected a fresh cigarette.

"You!" Rose's tone was almost as dry as his own.

"Indeed?" His eyebrows lifted. "And what did the *signora* wish to know about me?"

"Oh, all sorts of things," being deliberately casual. And then, more incisively: "She wished to know about Heather Willoughby!"

"I see." He stared at the tip of his cigarette. "And did you tell her about Heather?"

"No." She shook her head. "I regarded the question as impertinent."

"You know, Rose," Sir Laurence told her, regarding her through a faint haze of tobacco smoke which lingered heavily in the warm air between them, "you're extraordinarily adult in some ways, and quite, I should say, incorruptible. However, perhaps I'd better tell you a little bit about Lola. She's had some rather tough experiences in her own life — an extremely unhappy marriage amongst them—and when people have suffered similarly to oneself it's a kind of bond. It draws them together. Do you understand what I mean?"

Rose, looking down rather primly at the skirt of her dress, made a slight negative movement with her head which caused a twinkle of amusement to appear suddenly in his eyes.

"I see you don't," he murmured. "I also feel strongly that you would like to deliver another lecture to me on the subject of undesirable women friends, not one of whom you seem to approve. For you don't like Signora Bardoli any more than you liked Heather, do you?"

In spite of a suddenly heightened colour, Rose's clear eyes looked directly at him.

"Your women friends are nothing at all to do with me," she answered, with a suspicion of primness in her voice, "but I don't think you're particularly clever at choosing them. However," more hastily, "*that* is an impertinence on my part, and I apologize for it."

"You don't have to Rose." He sighed suddenly. "Out of the mouths of babes, you know! . . . But

118

I'd like you to know that Signora Bardoli is not a—replacement—for Heather! I'm not the type to rush blindly out of the frying-pan into the fire, you know!" He crushed out his cigarette in an ash-tray at his elbow. "At least I hope not!"

But Rose looked at him a little doubtfully, for there was such a thing as the frying-pan catching up with one, or the fire proving irresistible. And Signora Bardoli was not by any manner of means the same type as Heather Willoughby. Whatever she had suffered as the result of an unhappy marriage, she was a woman who knew what she wanted.

The conversation lapsed after this, and Sir Laurence looked rather thoughtful, while Rose tried to pick out the details in the magnificent panorama that was spread out before her. And then, with a look of apology for allowing her to feel temporarily neglected, her former guardian suggested driving her out to the Villa d'Este, which everyone on a visit to Rome went to see at least once. And as Rose had not so far seen it she was delighted with the beauties of this typical Roman villa, spread out over the heights of the Campania, with its centenarian cypresses and exquisite gushing fountain that was a joy to the eye. Between the silhouettes of the giant cypresses Rome looked blue and vague in the distance, and she was happy to wander there in the sunshine with the man who still seemed unusually preoccupied, or so she thought.

On their return he asked her, as he had done once before, whether she was in a hurry, and when she confessed that she was not, because Mrs. Wilson-Plunkett was spending the whole of the day with her friend, he suggested going back to the flat for a drink.

"It won't seriously compromise you, Rose" he told her, "any more than it has already done!"

119

But, back at the flat, he put a drink in her hand and then stood looking down at her. She had the feeling that he had made up his mind about something.

"Rose," he said rather slowly, and she felt a pulse beating nervously in her throat as his eyes held hers, "this morning we discussed Mrs. Wilson-Plunkett's plan for your future. It's not one I approve, because I believe I know you rather well, and somehow I can't see you—fitting into it very well!"

Rose felt suddenly indignant because he was talking as if she was the type who would allow someone to plan her future for her, and that was the very last thing she intended to allow anyone to do.

"I think—" she was beginning, but he made a little gesture which required her to be silent for a moment.

"Would you care to listen, Rose, to *my* plan for your future?" he asked.

CHAPTER XII

ROSE sat up almost nervously in her chair. Sir Laurence had been pacing up and down the room, with its cool light wood furniture and restful hangings, and single bowl of rather skilfully arranged flowers on an occasional table at her elbow. But when he saw the faintly alarmed, faintly anxious look which leapt into her revealing eyes he drew up a chair near to her.

"Rose, I'm not at all happy about the life you're living at the moment! I'm quite sure Mrs. Wilson-Plunkett is tremendously fond of you — I noticed that she took a great fancy to you almost immediately you arrived at Farnhurst Manor — but I don't think she's the right type to guide and advise you. Although you look quite a grown-up young woman, you're really awfully young, and . . ."

He broke off and smiled at her.

"I'd hate it if anything went wrong for you, Rose! I've known you since that hair of yours was in pigtails, and now that you wear it short and fashionably styled you seem to me even more vulnerable now than you did then!"

Rose looked at him for a long moment, and then away.

"It's good of you to concern yourself about me," she said rather stiltedly, "but I assure you it isn't necessary. As I told you that afternoon when we had tea in Rington—do you remember?—I'm quite capable of looking after my own future."

"Are you? Are you really, Rose?" But he sighed and look doubtful. He picked up one of her slender hands and examined it as if its delicate perfection actually temporarily fascinated him.

"Rose, do you look upon me as a—well, as very much older than yourself? Dully middle-aged, shall we say?" smiling with a kind of ruefulness.

"No, of course not." But she deliberately removed her hand and kept it firmly clasped round her other in her lap. "I've never thought of you as old—not even when—when I was younger!"

"Haven't you?" regarding her searchingly.

She shook her flaming head.

"And in any case you're not old. You're not yet middle-aged."

"But if I asked you to marry me, and you accepted, people could talk of May and December, couldn't they?"

"*Marry* you?" She was so startled that she actually sat bolt upright in her chair, and he looked at her with a still more rueful smile on his lips.

"Does the idea appal you?"

"I can't think you know what you're—talking about!" she answered.

But he assured her that he did. He assured her that he had given the matter a great deal of thought.

"I want to look after you, Rose, and I want to make certain that there are no disillusionments waiting for you in the years ahead! Oh, I know that you haven't yet fallen properly in love, and that there is probably a Mr. Right waiting for you around the corner—but he might not turn out to be *Mr. Right* after all! He might so easily turn out to be *Mr. Wrong!* And having survived a bitter experience myself, I couldn't bear it for you!"

"Why not?" Rose asked through distinctly dry lips.

"Because I'm fond of you, child—because . . ." He looked at her very earnestly, surprised because she had actually turned a little white, and her eyes looked enormous. "Because I'm *very* fond of you! Because I don't like the thought of you drifting about in this insecure fashion, and I know you love Enderby, and I think we could settle down there quite happily once we—made up our minds!"

"I see," Rose said, and her voice sounded utterly flat.

He sought to rally her, believing that he had merely taken her very much by surprise.

"And think of the amount of protection you could provide me with against these various females you so strongly disapprove of—like you, I wouldn't any longer be in any danger, would I?"

"No," Rose agreed, her voice trembling a little, "I suppose you wouldn't."

But she felt all at once that a flood of daylight had been poured out all over her, and his real reasons for asking her to marry him—*marry* him!— became almost lucidly clear. She knew she never would believe that something she had dreamed about was coming her way, and that she was turning it down. He really wanted protection from women like Signora Bardoli, he no longer trusted himself with the Heathers of this world, and he wanted to go back to Enderby and settle down. He could salve his conscience about her, Rose— let the world see that he was no longer breaking his heart over Heather—feel absolutely safe from Lola Bardoli, and be free to give his time to the work he really loved above everything else, if he settled everything out of hand by marrying her, whom he knew reasonably well, and of whom he admitted he was very fond!

"I'm sorry," she said, trying not to speak huskily, as if emotion was tearing at her, "but I couldn't ever consider anything of the sort!"

He allowed her to rise somewhat hastily from her chair and wander out on to the balcony, where they had drunk their coffee after lunch, and he watched her for a few moments leaning against the balcony rail. Then he followed her.

"Are you quite sure about that, Rose?"

"Quite sure," she answered without turning her head.

"Are you by any chance in love with Camillo de Lippi?"

"No,"giving her head a quick shake.

"Prince Paul de Lippi? Although he *is* too old for you!"

"I hardly know him," she answered this time.

"Then is there"—smiling a little wryly while she watched the sunset light gilding all the spires of Rome—"someone else I know nothing at all about?"

She turned and looked up at him gravely.

"There isn't anyone."

He put his hand on her shoulder and looked down at her very gently.

"In that case—won't you take time and think about it, Rose? Of course, I didn't expect you to make up your mind at once, and I know I'm not offering you a very romantic proposition, but ... You don't dislike me, do you? Shall I admit that I used to think you were rather fond of me?—perhaps especially fond! But that, of course, was before you became a very fashionable young woman, with all the world at your feet!"

"It isn't at my feet, as you very well know," she whispered chokily; and his hand slipped from her shoulder and went beneath her chin and lifted it.

"And do you still like me—a little?"

"Of course."

But she kept her eyes determinedly lowered.

"In spite of the harsh things I said to you once?"

"I don't believe you really meant them."

"No, I didn't. But it was true that Heather objected to you rather strongly."

His eyes dwelt thoughtfully on the delicate outline of her soft red lips.

"Do you know, Rose," he said suddenly, in rather a curious voice, "in all the years that we've known one another I've never kissed you! But I think I'd like to do so now, even if you won't marry me!"

And before she had time to do more than send a rather panic-stricken upward glance at him he bent his sleek head and she felt the cool, hard pressure of his lips against her own. There was so little of the violence, or the ardour, of Camillo de Lippi's lips, when they had taken possession of her mouth, that she actually found herself, as she stared up into his eyes, making a comparison. And then he smiled and stroked her cheek.

"You're very sweet, Rose!"

"I—" she managed; and then, to her complete astonishment, he suddenly caught her right into his arms and kissed her again, and this time there was no doubt about the warmth of his lips, and when he released her, her face was flaming, and she was trembling like a leaf in a strong breeze deep down inside her.

Sir Laurence looked at her with strange, inscrutable eyes, and apologized.

"I had no right to do that, Rose. Will you overlook it on the grounds that the temptation was very great?" And then he glanced at his wristwatch. "And now I'd better take you back to your hotel," he added almost casually. "Otherwise Mrs. Wilson-Plunkett will think someone has abducted you."

They drove back to the hotel in almost complete silence, but just before they reached it he said:

"Think over my suggestion, Rose, and if you change your mind let me know. Because I'm not at all happy about you at the moment."

But Rose looked thoughtfuly down at her hands and returned no answer. And when they entered the hotel she was thinking, rather wretchedly:

125

"How could any self-respecting young woman accept a proposal of that sort, even if all her instincts urged her to do so? To have him at any price! . . ." Her lips were still tingling from their contact with his lips, and she asked herself bewilderedly: "But what sort of a proposal was it . . .?"

Sir Laurence left her at the lift, and she went up in it alone, and when she reached Mrs. Wilson-Plunkett's suite that good lady was drinking tea she had just ordered to restore her after a somewhat exhausting day, and looking full of momentous news.

"My dear," she exclaimed as soon as she saw Rose, "what sort of acutely embarrassing thing do you think has happened now? The sort of thing that only my god-daughter would be capable of! I'm so annoyed for all sorts of reasons that I'm really quite upset!"

"Why—what—what do you mean?" Rose asked, and waited with the curious conviction that something she was to find rather more than embarrassing—and perhaps even more than upsetting—was about to be disclosed to her.

"Heather! Heather Willoughby"—Mrs. Wilson-Plunkett poured cream into her cup and added too much sugar to prove her agitation—"is in Rome! She's staying in this hotel, with my cousin, Augusta Sims. They arrived today!"

"And Heather's—husband?" Rose asked.

"She hasn't got one, my dear!" stirring her tea vigorously. "I didn't tell you that that affair came to nothing, because I thought it was best to forget it."

126

CHAPTER XIII

ROSE sat down in a chair rather limply and looked at the overdressed elderly figure in front of her.

"You mean that—that Heather didn't marry Peter Hurst after all?"

"Perhaps luckily for her she changed her mind before ever they reached Folkestone, where they were planning to pick up a Cross-Channel steamer," Mrs. Wilson-Plunkett admitted. "Of course, Peter Hurst is quite impecunious, and why she picked on him in preference to a man like Sir Laurence I can't think, but obviously some whim seized hold of her. However, she regretted it in time, and went back to Farnhurst, arriving just before I took my own departure. I knew she'd find another man soon—the Heathers of this world always do!—but the amazing thing is that she appears to be quite free at the moment."

"Does Sir Laurence know?" Rose managed, when her throat felt a little less dry. "I mean, does he know that she didn't marry?"

"Oh, of course. She wrote to him, I believe—some idea of patching things up obviously actuating her! But at that time he was no doubt feeling pretty sore, and he no doubt turned her down out of hand."

"Do you think he had any idea that she—intended coming to Rome?"

"Well . . ." The sharp-eyed old lady was looking at Rose rather curiously, and it struck her that the girl was displaying all the symptoms of having received something in the nature of a shock. "If you can believe anything Heather says, yes! I met her downstairs in the main lounge when I came in about an hour ago, and she and Augusta

127

wanted me to join them for sherry, but I don't touch anything like that so early in the afternoon, as you know. But Heather was quite uninhibited about all that had happened to her, and her plans for the future. She mentioned Sir Laurence's name quite casually, and knew that he had been staying in Rome for several weeks."

"But did she—write to let him know she was coming?"

"My dear child!" Mrs. Wilson-Plunkett looked suddenly concerned. "Have you had a very exhausting day or something? You look quite washed out! Perhaps you'd better have a glass of sherry. Ring the bell, dear."

But although Rose rang the bell obediently it was not because she wanted the sherry.

"Did he know she was coming?" she insisted.

"I should say it's pretty certain he did. However, Rose, the concerns of my god-daughter and your Sir Laurence don't really touch us, and if he's weak enough to be got over by a pretty face and plausible words, well, then, I for one won't sympathize with him when he gets his second awakening. But he may have made up his mind that there isn't going to be any second awakening."

"That's what I think," Rose said, in such a low voice that the elder lady's none too sharp ears missed it.

"Well," Mrs. Wilson-Plunkett declared, "it will be interesting to see how everything works out, but for the moment the thing I want to do is change for dinner. Thank goodness we're having a quiet evening in the hotel. I don't think I could face up to too much excitement tonight."

But it was Rose who felt not so much excited as tensed when they went down to dinner, and it was she who first caught sight of Heather and her elderly female chaperon when they entered the dining-room. The chaperon was obviously a

very faded spinster—and Mrs. Wilson-Plunkett
had had a few words to say about her, and her
willingness to allow all her expenses to be paid
for her on an occasion such as this—but Heather
looked as strikingly attractive as she had always
looked. If regret had gnawed at her over the past
few months, it didn't show in her face, and there
was a certain light-hearted sprightliness in the
way she walked—a consciousness of admiring
eyes—as she moved to the table to which the
maitre d'hotel himself guided them. When she
was seated she looked about her with wide, china-
blue eyes, and all the lights in the huge room
seemed to be concentrating their attention on her
spun-gold hair.

Rose sat watching her, feeling amazed that any
woman could have behaved as she had behaved
and be as content and unconcerned as she appeared in those moments. Her dress was probably one
of her trousseau dresses, for it was very lovely,
and obviously expensive, and every detail of her
grooming was perfect.

She must have sensed eyes on her, for suddenly
she looked up and across the whole width of the
room, and saw Rose. She smiled affably, casually,
and Rose was further amazed.

After dinner the quartette met as if it had been
arranged beforehand, and had their coffee together, and Heather was gracious and charming to
Rose.

"So you've got yourself a nice little job," she
said. "A job drifting comfortably around the
world with my god-mother! Well, if it suits you—
although I think I'd personally find it a bit dull—
and she pays you a good salary, that's splendid.
You look as if the salary is adequate anyway,"
taking in the details of Rose's simple white dress.

Rose didn't know how to reply to this, and she
felt a curious aversion to talking to Heather at
all. Every time she thought of what she had done

to Sir Laurence, and remembered that dreadful wait at the church, a bleak feeling of hostility which she had to fight against hard welled over her.

Heather probably gathered the lines along which she was thinking at last for she remarked with a rather brittle smile:

"I suppose you're one of the people who think I behaved badly? You were terribly devoted to Lance weren't you? And you were also nearer to him than anyone else. Was he—would you say—*very* upset when I went off like that?"

Rose, who had never expected to be asked such a question by the woman who had, in almost an unimaginative fashion, gone out of her way to wreck a man's life, swallowed something in her throat before she answered:

"What do you think? How would *you* have felt if the rôles had been reversed?"

"You mean if Lance had walked out on me?"

"Yes."

"Well, to begin with"—smiling with a good deal of complacence—"Lance would never have done a thing like that, and to go on with, I didn't do it to hurt him. I *had to* do it—at least I thought I had. I imagined I was in love with Peter, which, of course, I wasn't, and it's possible I was suffering, too, from those last-minute nerves and indecision which I believe quite a lot of brides go through before they reach the altar. And the fact that I didn't reach the altar was my mistake."

Rose was silent, and Heather looked at her curiously.

"Now that you're earning your own living, do you still keep in touch with Lance? Does he approve of your working like this?"

"It isn't exactly working, and—he was never my official guardian, as I think you know!"

"Yes, I did know." Heather laughed coolly. "It was one of the things that annoyed me extremely.

130

I thought you were a burden thrust on him! However," smiling in her new, affable fashion, "quite a lot of water has passed underneath the bridges since those days, and maybe we would have got on quite well together." She selected a fresh cigarette, and during the delicate operation of lighting it leaned a little towards Rose. "Tell me," she requested, "do you think I've got a hope of winning him back?"

As Rose looked as if the question had finally been too much for her, she held up an amused hand and stopped her answering.

"It's all right, my dear! I can see you're still very Lance-conscious, but I shall be seeing him myself very soon now, and if I really want him back it's up to me to get him, isn't it? The thing I was afraid of was that somebody might have caught him on the rebound, but somehow I don't think that has happened."

Rose felt as if she was in danger of choking with revulsion, and as the result of emotion which she had to keep very carefully bottled up; and it was a great relief to her when she discovered that she was being paged, and learned that she was wanted on the telephone. When she returned to the lounge Mrs. Wilson-Plunkett looked at her with interest and asked for the name of her caller, and when Rose admitted it was Prince Paul de Lippi, the rich widow's dyed curls started to bob with pleasure, and the lines of her face creased with infinite satisfaction.

"And what did he want, my dear?" she asked Rose.

"He would like me to have lunch with him tomorrow," the girl answered.

Mrs. Wilson-Plunkett's beam expanded.

"At the villa?"

"I think so. He has just bought some new pictures, and he would like me to see them. Some pictures and—other things," she added vaguely, because Heather was looking at her with very wide eyes indeed.

"Then I hope you accepted, child?"

"I said I didn't think you would mind."

"Mind?" The old eyebrows arched. "At what time is he calling for you?"

"About noon."

Later Rose pleaded a headache, and escaped to her room, and as soon as she had left them Heather turned to her god-mother and asked:

"Who is this Prince Paul de Lippi?"

"He is one of the most eligible widowers in Rome," Mrs. Wilson-Plunkett answered her very deliberately, and quite obviously with a certain amount of relish. "Rose has had a very noticeable effect on him, and as a matter of fact she's had almost a devastating effect on quite a few people since we left England. She's remarkably attractive, as even you must recognize, and I'm afraid I shan't have her as a companion for very long."

"I see," Heather observed, and her lips seemed to grow rather thin as they pursed themselves together.

The next morning, shortly before noon, Heather descended to the courtyard of the hotel where Rose, anxious to escape the others, had been spending very nearly a full hour, waiting for Prince Paul. She was seated on a white-painted seat near the coolness of the fountain, wearing faultlessly tailored ivory silk, with a shady hat partly concealing the splendours of the curling red hair.

When Prince Paul drove into the courtyard in his ivory and black car she stood up at once to greet him. Heather watching from the shadows of the hotel porch, saw the slight, elegant figure alight, a dark head that shone in the sunshine bent above Rose's hand, and flashing white teeth as the "eligible widower" looked down into an extraordinarily attractive face.

Heather realized that she was frowning, but the frown disappeared like magic when another car drove into the courtyard, and she recognized Sir Laurence Melville behind the wheel. He was wearing a light grey suit which fitted him perfectly, his hair was a rich brown in the sunshine, and instead of looking as if he had suffered a great deal he was actually looking a little younger than when she saw him last—although this effect had only been acquired during recent weeks. Heather, however, was not to know this, and the thing she did notice about him particularly was that he frowned quickly when his eyes lighted upon Rose and her Prince.

Rose felt her heart miss a beat when she turned to greet him, but the Prince was looking very sleek and satisfied, in a high-bred Roman manner, and not at all as if the arrival of Sir Laurence on the scene affected him one way or the other.

"Miss Hereward is doing me the honour of lunching with me," he said, as Sir Laurence looked at them both a little questioningly. "I have just unearthed a couple of delightful Tintorettos, and I am anxious to have her opinion on them." He beamed at Rose as if her opinion on any subject really was of considerable importance to him, and then held open the door of his car. "I do hope I haven't kept you waiting. I endeavoured to be as early as possible."

"I was hoping to have a few words with you, Rose," Sir Laurence said, as Rose made to step into the car.

She looked at him in a way that was new to him, for it was a look that was remote and withdrawn.

"I'm afraid I can't spare the time now. I expect I shall be seeing you again quite soon."

"This evening? Could I see you this evening—?"

And then Heather stepped forward gracefully from the shadows of the porch, and Sir Laurence seemed actually to stiffen for a few moments. His face, following an instant of astonishment, looked fixed and inscrutable.

"Lance!" she exclaimed, and held out a hand to him. Rose felt as if the breath was temporarily suspended in her throat as she saw that hand, and then she looked away as she heard Heather's melting tones. "I hoped we would meet soon! . . . I've only just arrived in Rome!"

The Prince put Rose into his car, and then bowed very correctly to Heather. She spared him one of her most brilliant smiles, and said softly, when Sir Laurence had made a hasty introduction:

"I'm delighted to meet any friend of Rose's! I'm sure she's going to have a very pleasant lunch! . . ."

And then the car was moving noiselessly away, and Rose, without turning her head, had a curiously vivid impression of Sir Laurence standing and looking after them, while Heather rested a hand—that same white, scarlet-tipped hand that had come out so eagerly to greet him—almost pleadingly on his sleeve.

Rose was never afterwards very clear how that lunch—her first alone with Prince Paul, for Camillo was in Florence—went off, but she did know that it went off very smoothly, and that the Prince was a perfect host. He seemed to attribute her slight air of reticence and preoccupation to natural shyness at being alone with him, and did his utmost to set her at ease, and be charming to her in almost a fatherly fashion. He showed her treasures at the villa that she had not seen before, including the pair of recently purchased Tintorettos, and conducted her through many of the rooms, so that she could admire them and be impressed by their magnificence. He had, she realized, impeccable taste, and his love of the beautiful and the antique was undoubtedly quite genuine. Under ordinary circumstances she could have shared it with him, and even enthused a little in her shy way; but all she could think of while lunch lasted, while they sipped liqueurs and drank coffee in a huge loggia with an outlook over paved paths and massed blooms to those fascinating dark shapes of cypress trees, rising against the intense blue of the sky, was Sir Laurence, as she had seen him last, with Heather's hand resting pathetically on his sleeve.

No doubt, once the car was out of sight, Heather had made an abject apology. Implored him to forgive her. Her whole expression had registered appeal—gentleness, compunction. She was ready to go to any lengths to convince him that she bitterly regretted what she had done, and since he had undoubtedly been very much in love with her once—whatever he had recently had to say about there being "degrees" of love—he would surely find it difficult to resist her in this new mood of penitence.

But that wasn't the only thing Rose thought about. She was certain, as Mrs. Wilson-Plunkett plainly was, that Sir Laurence had known about Heather's visit to Rome, and that while he was entertaining Rose to lunch the day before he had been very well aware of it. He had no doubt thought about it a great deal while they had lunch, and while they afterwards wandered in the grounds of the Villa d'Este. And because he couldn't trust himself, and felt the need of some sort of protective armour, had asked Rose to marry him!

He had even admitted, jokingly, that she could provide him with protection . . . But the one thing Rose hadn't altogether understood was that he was not merely joking! He had probably been quite in earnest!

When the Prince deposited her outside her hotel shortly before tea-time she thanked him, and he looked a little more meaningly into her eyes as he said his farewells. He also told her that he was giving a dinner-party to which Mrs. Wilson-Plunkett had already accepted invitations for them both a few nights hence, and that any time she wished for a car to be placed at her disposal she had but to telephone the villa. He made it clear that she could call upon him for anything that would make her stay in Rome more pleasant and thanked her for the great pleasure her company had given him.

Sir Laurence made no further attempt to get in touch with her that night, but at dinner Heather, she thought, looked even more complacent than the night before. When they foregathered in the lounge afterwards she provided no account of her day, but Mrs. Wilson-Plunkett told Rose that she had not been in to lunch, and Augusta Sims had had to lunch alone.

The following morning Rose went shopping early, with some commissions to execute for Mrs. Wilson-Plunkett, and she had no idea whether Sir Laurence called at the hotel or not for no one appeared to have seen him. In the afternoon Mrs. Wilson-Plunkett insisted on hiring a car and driving her out to meet the friend who had rented a villa on the outskirts of Rome, and when they returned, Heather, beautifully dressed for the evening, was just about to whirl through the glass doors and outside to a waiting taxi. Miss Sims announced plaintively that the girl she was supposed to keep a very watchful eye on had met an old friend in Rome, and was dining with him. But Mrs. Wilson-Plunkett's eyes, as they sought out Rose's, declared openly that she, at least, was not deceived by this.

If Heather had met an old friend it was a man who was only too conscious of being a fool to wish to call for her at the hotel and meet the surprised looks of people like Mrs. Wilson-Plunkett and

Rose, who knew just how badly she had treated him in the past.

"But I'll admit I'm a bit surprised," Mrs. Wilson-Plunkett said as they sat over sherry before going in to dinner. "Although it only goes to prove how weak the strongest man can turn out to be when a clever woman gets a tight hold of his emotions! And Sir Laurence is certainly a strong man, but Heather, apparently, is Heather!"

Rose, as they went in to dinner, hardly knew whether to despise Sir Laurence or to pity him. But she did know that she despised herself, and she was determined, if it was humanly possible, to outgrow her weakness where he was concerned.

The following morning she again went out early, but this time she wandered about Rome with only half a mind on its architectural splendours, and the other half in an almost numb state. She kept her eyes averted from every passing vehicle in case she should recognize Heather being driven in Sir Laurence's sleek Bentley, and in the tiny square which echoes with the exuberant music of the Fountain de Trevi stood looking at the coins in the basin, and resisted a childish impulse to add yet another one to their number and make another wish.

What good were wishes when there wasn't the remotest chance that they would come true?

As she wended her way back to the hotel she wished that Camillo had not gone to Florence to transact some business for his uncle, and that she would find his bright blue car standing outside the hotel. For she liked Camillo enough to be capable of finding a certain amount of diversion in his company, whereas, in the company of his uncle, it was not so easy to relax. She was not conceited enough to share Mrs. Wilson-Plunkett's belief—which was probably no more than wishful thinking—that he was seriously interested in her, but he did treat her in rather a special way which alarmed her when she was alone with him, because under no circumstances could she marry a man with whom she was not in the least in love.

Particularly when she was in love with another man! . . . a man who had kissed her lips lightly and casually because the sight of them had suddenly tempted him!

She walked fast back to the hotel, wishing she could blot out the memory, and she was almost relieved when she went up to their suite to find that Mrs. Wilson-Plunkett had made up her mind to rest that day (the Prince's dinner-party was the following night!) and was having lunch sent up to her in her own room. That meant that Rose was able to avoid the dining-room also, and the sight of Heather's satisfied face as she spooned her soup, and she had a light snack sent up to her in the sitting-room. Afterwards she spent an hour or so reading to Mrs. Wilson-Plunkett, and writing a few of her letters, and shortly before tea she took them down to the vestibule to post. She had just slipped them in the box reserved for visitors' mail, and was turning back towards the lift when Heather came quickly through the entrance, followed by Sir Laurence. Outside, through the glass doors, Rose could see Sir Laurence's car standing in the courtyard.

Heather was wearing powder-blue and white, and she had an enormous white pouch handbag underneath her arm. Her delicate complexion was lightly flushed and her eyes bright. She called out gaily to Rose as the latter turned:

"What! No princes around today? You must feel neglected!"

Her voice was mocking, for ever since she had discovered that Rose was receiving a certain amount of attention in Rome, and was far better dressed than she remembered her, she had obviously thought twice about her decision to be friendly.

"Good afternoon, Rose!" Sir Laurence's voice was cool, and even a little curt. "I began to think you and Mrs. Wilson-Plunkett had left Rome! Whenever I called or telephoned you were neither of your available to either see me or listen to me!"

Rose looked up at him as if she was taken slightly aback.

"I didn't know you—you had called!"

"Well, I did! I told you when the Prince was taking you out to lunch that I wanted to talk to you. Can you spare me a few moments now?"

Heather looked at them both with an odd gleam in her eyes.

"You obviously don't want me around," she said, "but if you're going to deliver Rose a lecture, Lance, be as gentle as possible! Remember, we're only young once!" She waved an airy farewell ere she moved towards the lift. "And thank you so much for the drive!"

Rose felt as if something rose up in her throat and made an attempt to choke her. He had just taken Heather, who had treated him so appallingly, for a drive, and at the same time he expected her, Rose, to be constantly available whenever he wished to see her.

She swallowed the indignation that had caused an actual lump in her throat, but her eyes flashed the most unusual green fire at him.

"I can't think what you wish to talk to me about," she said, "but since you apparently do wish to talk to me about something, we had better find somewhere quiet. The writing-room is usually pretty empty at this hour of the day."

She led the way to it like an affronted, red-headed duchess, and Sir Laurence followed with a frown on his face. The writing-room, when they reached it, was empty, and he shut the door closely to ensure greater privacy.

139

"You look offended, Rose," he remarked. "Have I done anything to offend you?"

"No, of course not." But her sensitive face flushed as she looked into his eyes. "However, you can hardly expect me to be always on hand whenever you wish to see me, and I resented the way in which you spoke to me in front of Miss Willoughby. You must remember you are not any longer my guardian."

"I'm not in the least likely to forget it," he assured her, the line of his lips looking suddenly rather thin. "You have made it increasingly plain to me that you don't wish me to interfere at all in your life! But the other day, when we had lunch together and spent the whole of the afternoon together as well, you were not in this strange, hostile mood. Has it anything to do with the suggestion I made to you, or has it something to do with the sudden arrival on the scene of Miss Willoughby?—as you always preferred to call her?"

Rose felt slightly taken aback by this direct method of questioning, but she refused to lower her eyes.

"When you made that suggestion to me the other afternoon," she counter-questioned, "did you know that Heather was on her way to Rome?"

For an instant she could have sworn that his amazement was genuine. And then such a bleak, hard, cold look overspread his face, followed by nothing short of a wall of inscrutability and reserve, that it actually filled her with a faint feeling of apprehension, and she didn't know what to think.

"I see!" he exclaimed. "So that's what you think, is it?"

She felt the colour burning more painfully into her cheeks and her eyes looked both uncertain and appealing.

"But you did know she was coming, didn't you? You knew that she hadn't married, and that she was still free, and you said yourself that you needed protection from undesirable females! I thought at the time you were joking—I've never thought you weak, but . . . but Heather is—Heather's the woman you were going to marry . . ."

"And, of course, I'm still violently in love with her?"

"I don't know very much about love," she admitted, pushing back a strand of her hair with rather a pathetic gesture, and looking at him with a young, confused gleam in her eyes. "But I shouldn't think that—that it could die quite so quickly—not if it really was love, as everyone thought at the time . . ."

"Oh, did they?" looking icily interested. "Including you, of course? In spite of the fact that you'd only just left school!"

"I was nineteen," she answered quietly, "and it seemed pretty obvious. You allowed her to do exactly as she liked with you, and she flirted outrageously right under your eyes. But you never seemed to mind! You never seemed to mind anything that she did, or how closely she often came to actually humiliating you," with that faint note of scorn creeping into her clear voice that had crept into it before when she had addressed him on this same subject. "But I wished many times that you were not so blind."

"For a nineteen-year-old you appear to have been extraordinarily observant," he remarked, looking a little pale and taut, but with a coldly humorous look round his mouth. "Quite remarkably observant! And I suppose you were certain that my awakening was as inevitable as the four seasons, and just a question of time?"

"I didn't expect it to happen—when it did happen!" she answered in a voice that was suddenly very low.

"No, and I don't suppose any of the others who were looking on you—like you!—and seeing most of the game, as people apparently do at a time like that, expected it, either! That was an unrehearsed effort, wasn't it?"

His smile was harsh and cynical, and all in a moment her heart contracted with pity for him, and some of it must have been given away by her eyes. For he suddenly put her on her guard by asking curiously:

"Why were you so concerned about me at that time, Rose? Why did you so particularly wish I wasn't so blind?"

She looked at him for a moment as if he had startled her, and then she looked away.

"I suppose it was because I—I was fond of you," striving so hard to sound quite casual about it that she actually sounded a little prim. "I always have been fond of you . . . You've been so good to me, and kind."

"And you felt much as you would have felt if you'd seen your father making an unwise marriage?"

"Y-yes, I expect so . . ."

"Or your brother, shall we say?" a little more dryly. "Since I don't think I'm quite old enough to be your father!"

Rose looked at him rather helplessly, and he looked back at her with a strong tinge of mockery.

"In any case, there are years between us, and your concern for me couldn't have been actuated by feelings any warmer than that! I accept that, especially as you looked almost startled when I asked you to marry me the other day!"

He started to pace up and down the room, and then he stopped and faced her again, his expression quite unrevealing.

"And I suppose you've quite made up your mind that, as Heather has come back into my life, my hopeless love for her has been revived, and everything is more or less as it was between

142

us? You could be right, of course, for there are very few of us who benefit from the lessons in our past—even the most salutary lessons!—and a man in love, as I'm sure you would agree, is a pitifully weak creature!" He shook his head at her. "Pitifully weak, I'm afraid Rose, so you'll be able to despise me afresh, and pour some more of that delicate scorn of yours over my head!"

Rose swallowed hard. For the life of her she couldn't tell whether he was merely mocking her or whether he was serious. And the fact that he had just brought Heather back to the hotel, that she had thanked him for the drive, and seemed to be on excellent terms with him, was surely an indication that he was serious!

And he had made no attempt to deny that he had known she was coming to Rome!

"So perhaps it's very fortunate that you refused to marry me the other afternoon, Rose, or even to consider marrying me, for things could have been a little awkward now that Heather and I have actually met again! You do see that, don't you?" He shot her an almost oblique glance and re-started his pacing up and down. "And, as it is, you can marry your Prince, and I'll marry Heather, and we'll both live happily ever afterwards, with no rude awakenings for either of us. Don't you agree?"

Rose tried to say something, but the words wouldn't pass her lips, and he smiled most peculiarly, she thought.

"Won't we?" he demanded. "And, from your point of view, a marriage to de Lippi will be a much safer thing than marriage to a man who would have used you as a barrier between himself and his various feminine entanglements! For anyone as beautiful as you are, Rose, and as sweet, that would be a poor outlook, and you were wise not to take it on—not even for the sake of Enderby!"

The sheer, harsh mockery, behind which lay a kind of harsher bitterness, in his voice, disturbed her all at once immensely, and she looked at him with sudden unconcealed anxiety to know what it was that he was trying to convey to her. But the coldness of his expression caused her to stammer painfully as she said:

"I hope very much that—that if you do think seriously of marrying Heather . . .—well, I hope you'll think about it a great deal before you finally make up your mind! In some ways Signora Bardoli—Signora Bardoli would be a safer person for you to marry! She—I'm quite sure she wouldn't ever let you down . . ."

"Thank you very much, Rose," he returned, with a kind of heavy gratitude in his voice. "It's immensely good of you to concern yourself with my love life, but I think I'll manage to sort it out by myself—left to myself!" He moved towards the door, and then turned and sketched her a kind of ironic little bow. "You've probably got an appointment for the evening, so I won't take up any more of your time."

"But there was something — something you wanted to say to me?" she reminded him, feeling desperately that she couldn't let him go like this.

"Was there?" His eyebrows arched. "Oh, yes, I wanted to know whether it would be out of place to offer you any congratulations? Whether, as a result of your lunch *pour deux* the other day, you and Prince Paul de Lippi have any glad tidings for your friends? Or is it Camillo, after all, who appeals to you most?"

Rose's hands locked and unlocked themselves as she stood there in front of him, feeling, and looking, a little pale—for the flush of embarrassment had faded right away from her cheeks. But her large, greeny-grey eyes were as inscrutable and unreadable as his own.

"If that was all you wanted to see me about," she said at last, "there wasn't really any necessity to call and telephone so often, was there?"

"On the contrary," he assured her cooly. "I wanted to be one of the first to congratulate you. My little Rose . . .! Taking such a stupendous step—I'm referring, of course, to marriage to the Prince, not Camillo, who wouldn't offer it— and perhaps having an unpleasant awakening herself one day!"

And then someone came and tried the door of the writing-room, and the interview had, perforce, to be broken up. Rose accompanied her ex-guardian out into the main entrance to the hotel, and then watched him striding through it and out to his parked car.

CHAPTER XIV

THE dinner at Prince Paul de Lippi's villa was all, and more, than Rose had felt certain she could expect, but there were more fellow guests than she expected, and somewhat to her relief Camillo had returned from Florence.

The Prince seemed to enjoy presenting Rose to the rest of his guests, and as she was wearing a dress of very stiff white taffeta that was an excellent foil for her colouring, and very youthfully simple at the same time, he had every excuse for feeling as if he was drawing particular attention to the latest acquisition to one of his delicate china collections, or some other rare trifle he was thinking of adding to the contents of the villa.

Indeed, as the evening progressed and he constantly drew her into the limelight, Rose had the feeling that he really was doing it deliberately, and Mrs. Wilson-Plunkett began to be comfortably certain of it. She beamed at Rose, told herself that it didn't matter if a man was twenty years older than the girl he proposed to marry when that girl was as striking as Rose—and therefore, the sooner someone took charge of her the better! —and when he was so rich that he could make up to her for his lack of youth by surrounding her with every comfort! To say nothing of turning her into a princess, which even in the year 1956 was still something!

Camillo was still looking, Rose thought, a trifle downcast, and when she accepted an invitation to accompany him outside for a breath of fresh air she discovered, as the result of judicious questioning, that he was feeling downcast.

Camillo admitted to her that he was in love with Francesca de Boccacello, but her mother expected her to marry well—which meant where she would be financially secure—and Camillo, if he ever did marry, would have to do so for much the same reason. Rose was shocked by a young man with his assets calmly resigning himself to doing without love in his life simply because, from his cradle, he had been accustomed to luxury, but she couldn't help sympathizing with him because, in his mood of dejection, and looking, as he did, almost devastatingly handsome, there was something about him that appealed to the maternal side of her.

When she suggested that his uncle, if he seriously wished to marry Francesca, might come to his rescue he looked at her sideways as if he wondered whether she quite realized what she was saying.

"My uncle—as you should know, Signorina Rose!—is planning to marry again, and although if he didn't I might inherit something from him some day (in fact I almost certainly would!), the lady he is proposing to marry is so very charming that I can quite understand his desire to add her," a little dryly, "to his collection of beautiful things!"

Rose looked at him rather sharply.

"His—collection of beautiful things?"

"Yes." He shrugged his shoulders slightly. "Do not let me disillusion you, Rose, but my uncle is a connoisseur first and foremost, and it is your looks that appeal to him above everything else! You have such a rare type of beauty, and there is something about you that calls out to be cherished and protected. My uncle would take a delight in cherishing you!"

"But," Rose said slowly, staring at the moonlit paths and the exquisite examples of garden statuary that showed up whitely in the same clear light, "I have no intention of marrying your uncle, Camillo."

147

"You—haven't?" For an instant she felt certain he did not believe her, and then while his dark, velvety eyes rested on her face, with its faultless bone formation and magnolia pale skin, its slightly drooping crimson mouth and downcast eyelids, an idea occurred to him. "It is the old *signora*—Mrs. Wilson-Plunkett—who would like you to marry him; but you—you are in love with someone! Is that it?"

Rose couldn't see any reason just then why she should deny the truth, and she made a faint inclination with her head.

"It is the tall Englishman—Sir Laurence Melville?" Camillo decided at once with sudden shrewdness.

Rose felt embarrassed because he had picked so immediately on the one man out of all the other men in the world whom she loved with the whole of her heart and soul.

"Sir Laurence was my guardian," she admitted a little falteringly, confusedly smoothing the skirt of her gown, "and I have always been very—well, I have liked him always!"

"And he? He still likes you very much, but not as anything more important than a—ward?"

Rose made another miserable inclination of her head.

"Then, in that case," Camillo said explosively, "the man is a fool! In fact he is worse than a fool —he is a blind ingrate! I don't mind telling you, Rose, that if you had ever displayed any tendency to fall in love with me, I would have asked you to marry me, and forgotten that I had very little to offer you!"

Rose smiled up at him gratefully.

"And Francesca?" she inquired softly.

He sighed.

"Francesca is, of course—Francesca! But what is the use of dwelling upon her"—he made a slight shrugging movement with his shoulders—"when

148

nothing can ever possibly come of it? We have known each other for years, and sometimes I think I am desperately in love with her, but at other times I am not—not quite so sure." He looked down into her face searchingly. "Why not forget this Englishman, Rose—forget that my uncle is planning to ask you to marry him—and try and pretend to yourself that you are just a little in love with me? The love might grow—in time it might be all that you would ask of life, and I would try and persuade my uncle to make sure— well, to make sure that we should never starve!"

"Then you do realize at last that I haven't any money at all of my own?" Rose asked, looking straight into his eyes and embarrassing him a little with the undeviating directness of that regard, and the knowledge which lay behind it.

He picked up one of her hands and played with the slender fingers, taking note of the fact that there was no emerald bracelet on her rounded wrist tonight.

"So you know I took you at first for a kind of heiress?"

"I was afraid that was what you did," she answered, very gravely.

He looked at her ruefully, and she smiled at him.

"It doesn't matter," she assured him, gently. "I never have had any money, and Sir Laurence paid for my schooling and all my expenses for years. He was my father's friend."

"And now you are in love with him?"

She looked away quickly.

"It's just the foolish thing that does happen sometimes in cases of this kind, but I've got to forget all about him and be sensible. He—"

"Don't tell me he is seriously interested in the Signora Bardoli?"

"No; but there is—someone else . . ."

"I see," he said, and squeezed her hand. Then he carried it ardently up to his lips. "Forget him,

Rose," he urged. "Forget him, say 'no' to my uncle—and marry me! I swear that I will make you a devoted husband, and love you for the rest of your life! I will even—if it should become necessary—work for you . . . !"

Rose couldn't resist the impulse to laugh suddenly and softly, with genuine amusement.

"Have you ever done any work in your life?" she asked.

"No, but I could try," grimacing a little.

She touched his face gently, a butterfly's caress, with her slim fingers.

"I like you enormously, Camillo," she told him, "but I couldn't bear to see you reduced to such a pass that you had to work in order to keep me! But I do thank you very much for—well, for asking me to marry you! Even if you might have regretted it later on!"

Her second proposal of marriage that night— much more serious this time—came just before the evening drew to an end, when she was walking in the garden with her host. He had not made any excuse to get her outside and away from the others—he had simply told her that he wished to speak to her alone. And in the same little marble pavilion where she had sat with Camillo, looking out across the night-enshrouded garden, with Rome spread out like an illuminated carpet in front of them, he asked her, with a great deal of formality, if she would do him the honour of becoming his wife.

He did not tell her that he loved her, or look at her with passionately devoted eyes; but he told her that he was most anxious to protect her and care for her, and that if she became his wife he would see to it that for the rest of her life she was absolutely secure. There would be no need for anyone like Mrs. Wilson-Plunkett to condescend to her, or any man like Sir Laurence Melville to imagine a right to interfere in her affairs.

She would have a husband to lean upon who would cherish her as he cherished all the gems in his priceless collections, with the slight exception —and this she gathered for herself, without having it put into actual words—that she would be rather more valuable than the other gems, and for that reason even greater care would be taken of her.

For a single instant, as this proposition was put to her, Rose found herself not actually tempted by the proposition, but inclined to wonder what it would be like if she yielded all at once to an extraordinary temptation to say "Yes." The beaming smiles of Mrs. Wilson-Plunkett would be a reward in themselves; the fact that in future no man such as Sir Laurence Melville could offer her marriage for some obscure reason of his own, that she would *have* to stamp out any feeling that she had for him, and that the Heather Willoughbys and Signora Bardolis of this world would no longer dare to look at her as if their instinct was merely to patronize her—and perhaps "use" her, if it suited them occasionally—were all, for that brief fraction of time, excellent reasons why she should grasp thankfully at such a proposal of marriage from a man in the unassailable social position of Prince Paul de Lippi.

But she knew, when the moment of temptation had sped on its way, that under no circumstances could she do anything of the kind. She explained this to the Prince, with the right amount of gratitude in her voice for the honour he had paid her, and although at first she was certain he was surprised, it was gradually borne in on him that she meant what she said. But even so, he declined to accept such an answer as final.

"I have taken you by surprise," he said. "I have given you very little real time to know me! But I can be patient! I will wait!" He smiled at her, very gently, in the fashion she liked, but which had so little to do with the smile of a lover.

"Yes, I will wait!" he repeated, and she wondered unhappily what Mrs. Wilson-Plunkett would say when she knew about this proposal of marriage, which she had undoubtedly worked for, being turned down.

It was on the way home, in the Prince's car, that Mrs. Wilson-Plunkett learned the worst. She looked at Rose as if she was certain she was crazy, but instead of appearing annoyed with her, she merely looked almost sad.

"You are more foolish than I thought, Rose," she told her. "You are behaving as I would have behaved when I was your age! I wanted love and romance—a passionate attachment which never actually came my way! But at least I've been secure, and my marriage brought me lasting things. You have turned down the sort of marriage that most girls would give their eyes for, and all because of a man who hadn't the sense to wait for you!"

"What—do you mean?" Rose asked, looking sideways at her in almost a frightened manner.

Mrs. Wilson-Plunkett made a sound like an actual snort of disapproval.

"Sir Laurence, of course! He's like so many men of his type—always confusing the issues! If life was an actual tapestry, the threads he would work into it would be all the wrong colour! Because he can't even distinguish black from white —pure gold from tarnished silver!"

Rose peeped at her for a more literal explanation, and the old lady gave her one.

"Sir Laurence looked after you for five years, and he should have known that there was something about you that would appeal to him violently one day, just as there's something about him that prevents you seeing any other man in his true colours. I realized that in those early days of our acquaintance, just before the wedding that never took place, and that was one reason why I

152

wanted to get you away and give you other things to think about that had nothing to do with a man who was wilfully blind! You're too good, Rose, for second thoughts—you should be a man's first thought and, if possible, his first love! But that, apparently, isn't the way you want it!"

She lay back against the luxurious upholstery looking suddenly a little tired, and all at once very old, and Rose felt almost guilty.

"I'm sorry," she said gently, "if I've disappointed you!"

"It doesn't matter, child." Mrs. Wilson-Plunkett sighed. "And it could be, of course, that you're right, and I'm the one who is confusing the issues. However, we'll find out about that one day—when the issues have settled themselves!"

And then she shut her eyes as if she didn't want to talk any more, and Rose found herself turning over in her mind just one thing she had said, and feeling certain it was not in the least true:

"Sir Laurence looked after you for five years, and he should have known that there was something about you that would appeal to him violently one day!"

She lay back quietly in her own corner and felt a kind of burden of depression wash over her as it suddenly struck her that out of three men she had got to know rather well not one of them felt in the least violently about her. There was Camillo, who was charmed by her and quite ready to fall lightly in love with her if she would encourage him to do so, his uncle who stopped short at admiring her, and wished to possess her because she pleased his artistic eye. And there was Sir Laurence, who thought about her as "Poor little Rose" and could not deny a sense of responsibility where she was concerned.

Rose decided miserably, in the star-pricked gloom of the car, that she almost certainly lacked

153

something—something vital to the igniting of a spark of more ardent need for her in a man's breast. By comparison with Heather she was both colourless and uninterestingly young.

She noticed that Heather very rarely made her appearance in the dining-room at lunch time, and that if she did appear at lunch she hardly ever appeared at dinner, and for the remainder of the evening she vanished completely.

Miss Sims seemed to be rather a poor sort of chaperon, considering that the Willoughbys were no doubt depending on her to make certain Heather made no more serious mistakes in her life, and for that purpose, and that purpose only, were paying all her expenses. She seemed to know less than nothing about Heather's comings and goings, except that a mysterious "old friend" was taking her about, and introducing her to the pleasures of Rome.

Rose, knowing so much, realized that she could have given a name to the "old friend" if she had wished. She was so certain of this that she even tried to reassure Miss Sims that there was nothing to worry about, and that Heather's parents would neither of them be alarmed if they knew what had happened to their daughter so soon after her arrival in Rome.

They would even feel whole-heartedly thankful that they had not quibbled at the expense, or decided that "a change for Heather" was not practicable at that stage, with such a mountain of expenditure only recently met behind them.

Sir Laurence did not make any appearance at the hotel, but one evening when they were looking on at the dancers after dinner she saw Signora Bardoli with a rather elderly escort whom she did not recognize.

The *signora* was looking as striking as usual, and her escort was plainly very attentive, and

Rose found herself watching them—remembering that night when she had first made the acquaintance of the Italian woman.

Mrs. Wilson-Plunkett was growing a little tired of Rome, and she was talking of going onto Venice for a few weeks before trying somewhere altogether fresh, and Rose had a sudden, almost dismayed feeling at the thought of leaving Rome without perhaps seeing Sir Laurence again. She was trying to conceal the fact that she was feeling a little sick with an anguish and an unhappiness that was growing worse lately, when she caught the *signora's* eyes upon her, and across the room those eyes signalled a desire to speak to her.

When, later, Rose was in the cloakroom, attending dispiritedly to her make-up, Signora Bardoli came up behind her and announced at once that she had followed her.

"I did not wish to join your party, but I was hoping very much for an opportunity to have a word with you." She came to the point at once. "When did you last see Sir Laurence?"

Rose admitted that she had not seen him for several days.

"In fact, since the Signorina Willoughby arrived he has avoided you, and you have avoided him?" The dark Italian eyes looked shrewdly at the pale face confronting her, with its rather wistful eyes. Rose had just added a touch of lipstick to her lips, but it was not very much use as protective armour. "I think you are rather stupid," the older woman said suddenly and very deliberately.

Rose looked at her in rather dull amazement.

"Stupid?"

"Yes."

The white shoulders rising out of a confection of silver lace shrugged slightly.

"Me, I am so much older than you that I have few illusions left, but I know when a man, in spite of past mistakes, is worthy of saving from the results of those mistakes! Sir Laurence doesn't take easily to being badly hurt, and once you have been badly hurt it is natural to become over-sensitive, and to imagine that even amongst those people you wouldn't normally suspect of a desire to wound you there is a tendency to wound, nevertheless! Perhaps Sir Laurence is a little unreasonable, and he has not stopped to think that you are very young—but what is it that you have done to him that has caused him to make up his mind suddenly and leave Rome?"

"I? Cause him to leave Rome?"

Rose sounded so uncomprehending, while at the same time she actually turned a little pale, that the *signora* put a friendly be-ringed hand and grasped her arm.

"Yes, my dear—when I saw him this afternoon he was already packing! Far from being interested in the arrival in Rome of that young woman he was to marry, he did, I believe, snub her the instant they met again, and she is now amusing herself with a very elderly, but wealthy, friend of my late husband's whom she met, I believe, a year or so ago! They have been seen all over Rome together, and if she is clever she may persuade him to marry her. But Sir Laurence—for Sir Laurence she will never again have any charms whatsoever, and that is why I say that you are stupid!"

"But I"—Rose fumbled with the clasp of her evening-bag, and looked very young and helpless, and badly in need of a certain amount of well-meant advice—"but the fact that Sir Laurence is leaving is nothing—nothing to do with me . . .!"

"Isn't it?"

Rose's face flushed.

"Well, how could it be? I haven't seen him for nearly a week, and in any case his movements were never dictated by anything I could ever do or say! He has only just stopped looking upon me as a schoolgirl, and he isn't very pleased with me because I—"

"Because he thinks you're going to marry Prince Paul?"

"But I'm not going to marry Prince Paul," with a sudden, very un-youthful dignity.

The Signora Bardoli looked interested.

"Then I think you should let Sir Laurence know that your mind is so definitely made up! And I think you shouldn't waste any time, because he is leaving his flat almost immediately. Tonight it would not perhaps be quite the thing for you to call upon him, but tomorrow morning you must catch him as early as you can." There was no real friendliness in the hard eyes that studied Rose, but there was a certain curious wryness in her expression. "You will understand that for your ex-guardian I have an—admiration, shall we say? It disturbs me that he should slip away from Rome and the friends he has made recently and do, perhaps, something rather rash! He has work to complete here—work that was beginning to absorb him—and it vexes me that it should be left uncompleted because—because you," with sudden harsh impatience, "are so very young . . . !"

Rose looked at her as if, in spite of her youth, she was beginning to have a faint glimmering of what the other was attempting to convey—astounding though that intelligence was—and deep down inside her her feeling of relief because Heather, apparently, had failed to recapture Sir Laurence was growing moment by moment.

Then he must have been mocking her that last time he came to see her . . . !

"Do you think," she asked, in a voice that persisted in trembling in spite of herself, because apparently much depended on her all at once, "that I can stop Sir Laurence leaving Rome?"

"I think," the *signora* answered, as harshly as she had spoken before, "that you can have a try . . . !"

CHAPTER XV

ROSE stepped out of the lift on Sir Laurence's floor and approached the front door of his flat. Her pulses were all hammering so noisily in her ears that she had the feeling that anyone who came close to her would hear them as well, and as she pressed the bell the colour slid away from her cheeks and she not only looked but felt pale as she waited for the front door to open.

She had very little time to wait, for almost immediately footsteps sounded in the hall, and Sir Laurence himself stood looking at her without making any attempt to conceal his surprise.

"I'm honoured, Rose," he remarked at last, and then stood aside for her to enter. She didn't dare to glance at his face, but she had an impression of arched eyebrows and rather coldly set lips. His voice was very dry as he invited her into his sitting-room.

Rose saw at once that the place seemed to be in a kind of uproar. The table was covered with papers which were obviously in the process of being sorted, a despatch-case stood waiting on a chair, a stack of books were ready to be thrust into a packing-case, and there were other evidences of intending departure in the general litter in the room. Through the open bedroom door she could see suitcases piled upon the bed and drawers standing open.

"Do sit down." He cleared a chair for her, and pulled it forward politely. It was his politeness that actually seemed to freeze her and caused her nervousness to increase. "It's so surprising to have you calling upon me, Rose, that you must forgive me if I seem a little taken aback!"

The extreme dryness of his voice made her wince.

"I—I heard you were going away . . ."

"Oh!" He sat down on the arm of a chair and gave a hitch to one of his carefully-creased trouser legs. "And how did you hear that?"

"Signora Bardoli told me!"

She saw him smile oddly.

"You and the *signora* seem to have become rather close friends! At least, you meet fairly frequently, and she was telling me yesterday that she quite admires you colouring! She also seems to be of the opinion that you're very young and inexperienced, and that you want someone to direct your path for you. I told her that Prince Paul de Lippi was planning to do that!"

Rose looked down at the clasp of her handbag and hoped he didn't notice that her hands were none too steady as she fumbled with it.

"Why are you going away?" she asked, ignoring what he had just said.

"Because I think I'm growing a little tired of Rome."

"But you were working on some particular plans! You—you wanted to complete them, and you said that Rome held something you didn't want to say good-bye to yet awhile," she reminded him

"Did I?" looking at her with almost cynical detachment. "Well, maybe it did when I said that, but you must remember that there are certain views, or aspects of a view, which pall rather suddenly after a time, and shall we say that I'm a little surfeited with all that Rome holds? I want to get away and seek pastures new."

"Then you are not planning to return to—Enderby?"

"I don't think so—not yet. But I shan't remain away from it very much longer." This time he looked at her with a kind of grimness. "You mustn't get the idea that I'm in the state of mind when I'm still looking for distraction! I'm not ...! I've learned my lesson, and I'm completely cured!"

"Yes," she said, moistening her lips after swallowing rather painfully. "I'm afraid I—I owe you an apology for what I said to you about—about Heather!" Her eyes appealed to him, but he didn't seem to be much moved by her appeal. "For the second time in my life I said things to you that I—had no business to say, and I don't suppose you'll find it very easy to forgive me? I know now that Heather—well, that it isn't you she has been seeing a lot of since she arrived in Rome, and that there was not really any danger of your being—attracted to her a second time! And I didn't really mean that you were—weak—even if you had been attracted ..."

"You're very good and very generous, Rose," he told her; but instead of the words reassuring her they filled her with a sudden cold sensation like despair once she had got over the shock of looking into his eyes. For they were cold and amused and hostile—so definitely hostile that she felt bewildered. "But in future there won't be any need for you to concern yourself about me, for I don't imagine we shall see very much of each other. Our paths will lie very widely apart, and when I said just now that I no longer needed distraction, and that I was completely cured of a weakness you have kindly decided never existed, I really meant that I no longer had any illusions about—anyone! Do you understand what I mean by that?' treating her to almost a contemptuous regard. "And very soon now I hope to go back to Enderby and take up my life where I left it off, and this time I shall fill it with the things that really matter. And here in Rome I've discovered that work matters, and that the more one has of it to occupy one's mind the happier one is! I don't intend ever again to be at the mercy of—human relationships! I'm the type of man to grow into a nice crusty old bachelor, but crusty or not, I shall be well content with what I have!"

"I see," Rose said, and stood up suddenly. She felt as if she was blundering in the dark as she made a little movement towards his door. "Well, then, I—it only remains for me to say how much I hope you'll find that contentment, and I—won't interfere with your packing!"

He looked at her with an unchanging expression in his eyes, but there was a rather hesitant note in his voice as he protested:

"But I haven't even offered you a glass of sherry! You were kind enough to visit me, too"—back on the note of derision—"and I haven't yet learned what you came for?"

"It wasn't anything important. Just to—well, as I heard you were going away, to say goodbye . . ."

"You didn't think I'd come and say good-bye to you?"

"I wasn't sure."

He smiled slightly.

"I hadn't quite made up my mind as a matter of fact," he admitted carelessly. "For one thing, I didn't know whether you could find time to see me, and for another I haven't a great deal of time myself. I'm flying to America by way of the Bahamas tomorrow morning, and I've still quite a lot of things to clear up here."

Rose suddenly felt so appalled—so horrified by the thought of the miles that would separate them after tomorrow—that she simply couldn't say anything at all, and he glanced at her curiously as he walked behind her to the front door.

"You have my solicitor's address, Rose, and the address of my bank—and if you want to get in touch with me at any time your letter will be forwarded. I should particularly like to hear when you're getting married, and then I can send you a wedding present."

But Rose heard herself say, as if she was talking in a dream, and therefore the words sounded curiously stilted:

"I'm not getting married—I never had any intention of getting married! And if I did I—wouldn't want any present from you!"

He frowned quickly, but his voice was still mocking as he said:

"Don't tell me the Prince didn't come up to scratch?"

"If you mean—did he ask me to marry him? Yes, he did," she answered mechanically, and opened the front door before he could reach it.

"Then I don't think you were very wise to refuse him, Rose!" But there was not quite so much inscrutability about his expression as he looked down at her, and it was even very faintly concerned. "What did Mrs. Wilson-Plunkett say?"

But Rose simply turned and held out her hand to him.

"Good-bye," she said, without looking at him.

He frowned more noticeably.

"You'd better let me drive you back to the hotel," he suggested, "or at least get you a taxi. If you'll wait here I'll telephone for one."

"I don't want a taxi," Rose answered, with a stubbornness in her voice that he had never heard before. "And I certainly wouldn't allow you to drive me back to the hotel! You have your packing to attend to, and I mustn't keep you. Good-bye," she repeated, snatched her fingers from his hold, and then darted towards the lift just as it ascended and the liftman invitingly held open the gates.

Sir Laurence strode after her and exclaimed, "Rose!" commandingly, but she said urgently to the liftman that she was in a hurry to keep an appointment, and the gates clanged and the lift descended before Sir Laurence actually reached it.

CHAPTER XVI

ROSE emerged from the flats and walked without realizing where she was going for nearly half a mile, and then she took a taxi back to the hotel. She only took the taxi because she suddenly recognized that she was in unfamiliar surroundings, and it was the only way to prevent herself from becoming completely lost.

Arrived at the hotel, she settled the fare fumbling, as if only half her mind was alert to what she was doing, in her handbag for her purse, and then went up to the suite she shared with Mrs. Wilson-Plunkett. But that good lady was in the hands of an Italian beauty expert who was making it more and more difficult for anyone to tell her age, and she was not expected back until some time in the afternoon.

Rose ordered a light sandwich lunch for herself to be sent up to the suite, discovered that there was a letter for her from Yvonne de Marsac, with whom she had kept up a fairly regular correspondence, and sat down to read it. Yvonne, while openly envying her all the delights of Rome, was full of excitement because at last she had obtained a really worthwhile job, and she had even found herself a tiny flat in which to live, and where she could be completely independent of her parents. The only snag was that the rent was rather high—but rents all over Paris were alarming, she assured Rose—and she wished she had someone to share it with her who would help reduce expenditure. If only Rose wasn't living in the lap of luxury, and was still looking for a job, how marvellous it would be if they could share the flat together!

This wistful conclusion passed Rose by—by no means in a state of mind when anything penetrated very deeply—until all at once, as if she was enveloped in a blinding flood of daylight, and a bell rang a kind of clarion call in her ears at the same time, she knew exactly what she must do.

She looked around her at the luxurious sitting-room, with its flowers and its costly personal trifles scattered about that did away with the impersonality of a hotel sitting-room. She went into her room next door and stood looking at her dressing-table loaded with toilet articles, and opened the door of her wardrobe and examined, as if she was seeing them for the first time, all her expensive dresses. She felt almost appalled by the amount of money that had been spent on her recently, with so little return for Mrs. Wilson-Plunkett. Not even the satisfaction of having cleverly contrived a highly satisfactory marriage for her protégée!

Rose felt almost sick with shame as the full realization of how much she had taken and how little she had given welled over her. She was genuinely devoted to Mrs. Wilson-Plunkett, and the latter undoubtedly gained a lot of pleasure from her constant society, and the little things she did for her, but to go on like that—to permit Mrs. Wilson-Plunkett to keep her in luxury indefinitely was suddenly unthinkable.

She thought of Yvonne, whose parents owned a huge but mouldering château south of the Loire, living in a tiny flat in Paris—probably something tucked away in a none too salubrious district, reached only by flights of stairs, and with smells of cooking dwelling always in the atmosphere around her—and told herself that if her old school friend could put up with that sort of thing so could she, Rose. She could break away from being sheltered and protected, and begin to fend for herself. It was high time she started to fend for herself, and the big mistake she had made was in allowing herself to be looked after by other people too long.

As she reached for a light suitcase and started to pack things automatically—just a change of underwear and some night attire, a spare skirt for her suit, and a couple of blouses—she wouldn't admit to herself that it was because she simply *had* to get away from Rome that she was doing this. She wouldn't admit that she was numb, dazed and confused, appalled by the thought of staying on in a city where everything would remind her of Sir Laurence, and where, after tomorrow morning, he would no longer even be living near her.

IIis flat would be empty, the key handed over to the caretaker or the porter, or whoever it was one handed keys over to when one lived in a block of modern flats, and his car would probably be on its way back to England, if he wasn't taking it with him to America. She wouldn't even see his car in the streets, flashing past occasionally along a broad thoroughfare.

And America! . . . The Bahamas, where he was once to have spent part of a honeymoon, and then America! . . . So far away that she gulped when she thought of it.

And when she thought of the way he had looked at her, the drip of ice in his voice each time he had spoken to her, the complete casualness of his manner when he said good-bye—although he had tried to stop her departing quite so abruptly—the lump in her throat assumed the proportions of something that could actually choke her, and her fingers shook as she fumbled with the locks of her case.

No; she would go right away . . . Mrs. Wilson-Plunkett would understand and forgive her in time! . . . She would leave a note asking her not to worry about her, and to let her know that if there was an afternoon plane to Paris she was going to catch it. She had just about enough money in her purse, with sufficient left over once she had brought her ticket to keep her for perhaps a week. And Yvonne would help her after that, she felt sure she would, if she was slow in obtaining employment . . . Yvonne wouldn't let her starve . . .

She went back into the sitting-room and wrote the note, leaving it in a prominent position, where Mrs. Wilson-Plunkett couldn't possibly overlook it. Then she looked at the lunch she had ordered to be sent up, decided that she couldn't touch the sandwiches on the tray, but poured herself a cup of half-cold coffee and drank it feverishly.

She took a last look round the sitting-room of the suite, and felt one solitary pang because she was leaving it—and that was only in connection with Mrs. Wilson-Plunkett, who had treated her with such excessive kindness and generosity. And then she went down in the lift, and outside the hotel she got herself a taxi.

Arrived at the airline offices, she again counted her money while she was waiting to be attended to in order to make certain that she really had enough for a ticket, and felt almost pathetically grateful when the information was conveyed to her that there was a last-minute cancellation on the afternoon flight to Paris, and that it was hers. She again got herself a taxi, and at the airport went through Customs formalities, the business of having her luggage checked and weighed, ticket inspected, and so forth, with the feeling that nothing that was actually happening to her was quite real, and that at any moment she might expect to wake up and discover that it wasn't real.

Once aboard the aircraft there was still no real feeling of kinship with her surroundings and none of the excitement one normally feels at undertaking a sudden journey; and the air hostess, after one or two shrewd looks at her, decided that she wasn't feeling particularly well, or that she was suffering from nervous tension, and as soon as they were airborne endeavoured to persuade her to drink a cup of coffee or tea. But Rose was quite certain now that she couldn't swallow anything—not even liquid—and she merely smiled her thanks rather wanly, and then tried to concentrate on some magazines.

Despite the air conditioning, it was very warm —Rome lay bathed in golden sunshine when they left—and the first hour seemed to pass very slowly. Rose grew tired of pretending that she could make any sense of the printed pages in front of her, and took to looking out through her window and studying the vague carpet of land over which they were flying. All around her the sky was very blue, the sunlight was a persistent hot dazzle, and at one time she saw blue sea below her. Then they were turning inland again, and making for the mountains, and her thoughts winged backwards to Lausanne and the far-away days when she had lived there for a whole year, and had— or so it seemed to her now—not a care in the world.

She felt nostalgia seize hold of her when she caught her first glimpse of the snow-capped peaks. She remembered how she had been taught to ski up in that guardian circle of mountains, and how exhilarating it had been, although she had never become a very polished performer. She was a little too timorous by nature for the hazards of a really exciting ski-run, although Yvonne de Marsac had never shown any fear of any kind. But Yvonne was like that about most things she found herself forced to tackle—eager, as she would put it, to "try anything once," not in the least afraid that it would be beyond her, fatalistic if by any chance something she attempted should turn out to be beyond her.

And very soon now Rose would see her again. They would be sharing that tiny flat in Paris, and

Yvonne wouldn't ask any questions, because she could be discreet when she chose—and in any case Rose would be too numb to answer. She would just say that she wanted to be more independent, that she wanted to have a real career. And perhaps in time she might be able to embrace some sort of a career. There were such things as nursing, child welfare, overseas organizations that looked after displaced persons, and where help was badly needed, for which she would not need to pay to train. Those were the sort of things that would really occupy her mind, and be much more rewarding than trying to be a secretary, or something of that sort.

She wasn't the type to make an ideal secretary. She wanted more human contacts . . .

The afternoon light became tinged with a warm redness as the sun westered and the snow peaks below her were tinged with red. They sparkled like the many facets of a diamond with a rosy arc-light concentrated on it.

Rose began to feel an utterly weary drowsiness overcoming her as she stared down as if fascinated through her window. The peaks didn't really seem to be so very far below her, and she could make out with ease the green valleys dropping away below the snow-line, and the forests of pine and juniper that clothed some of the slopes. There were toy-like houses, too—chalets, she remembered. But these were probably climbers' huts, and the green plateaux on which they stood were a vivid emerald in the slanting light.

She made out cataracts tumbling down the mountainsides, and actually saw one disappearing under a primitive kind of wooden bridge. She watched it, imagining the roar as it tumbled into the depths below the bridge, and then started to be vaguely puzzled by the fact that she was seeing so much detail.

She looked up with rather more alertness than she had hitherto shown that afternoon, and observed that the air hostess had just stepped through the door which led to the crew's quarters. She was very smart in her uniform, and her cap was worn at a jaunty angle on her beautifully dressed hair, but she seemed to be smiling rather an unnatural smile, or so Rose thought.

She looked about her at the other passengers, and saw that more than one of them was wearing a worried expression. And there was no doubt that they had lost a great deal of altitude and one of the engines seemed to be making a most unpleasant noise, while the propeller on the starboard outer engine had stopped dead. Rose felt her heart do a kind of uneasy little descent into her stomach as she noticed it, and then immediately, she reassured herself because there were four engines. Possibly it was customary to rest an engine sometimes, and if only one of the other three wasn't making such explosive noises, and they hadn't started to rock and sway as if the aircraft itself had quite suddenly become possessed she would have listened to her own reassurances.

But surely it was quite unlikely that an engine would be rested whilst flying over the Alps, and there was no doubt about it the air hostess, standing bracing herself against the door of the ladies' powder-room, was looking rather ghastly.

As the huge aircraft swung wildly, those appallingly sharp peaks below drew nearer, and the roar of the exploding engine practically deafened them, the trim young woman in uniform managed to request:

"Will you all please fasten your seat-belts! We've got to make a forced landing, but there isn't really anything to worry about . . .!"

Nothing to worry about . . .!

Rose looked downwards, swallowed, shut her eyes, and then opened them again. She watched the green valleys rushing up at her, realizing that the pilot was doing his utmost to straighten out his machine, find some piece of level land once he had negotiated the first of those sickening peaks—it swung past even as Rose, completely fascinated, looked—and perform the miraculous feat of bringing all his passengers safely in to land.

But Rose felt certain this was a feat he could not perform. But she felt a tremendous admiration for the supreme effort he was making just the same. And somehow she wasn't afraid—not in the way she had always imagined she would be afraid if anything like this ever happened to her. Perhaps it was because she had been so desperately unhappy until thus suddenly diverted and the effects of the unhappiness were like an anæsthetic that had destroyed all cute sensitivity, and she merely thought how utterly strange it was that her life should end like this.

In the way a drowning person reviews the whole of his life until the waves claim him, so she reviewed, in a brief, introspective flash, her last few weeks in Rome—Camillo and his bright blue sports car, lunches and dinners at the Villa de Lippi, Heather with a white pouch handbag underneath her arm, and wearing a powder-blue dress . . . The fountains of Rome, and particularly one into which she had thrown a coin. The wish she had made . . . Sir Laurence saying he was completely cured, and with no more illusions . . . Saying he was going back to Enderby! . . .

She heard a child start to cry on the other side of the aisle, and the shrill note of fear in the mother's voice as she attempted to soothe it. Another gigantic Alp slid past crazily . . .

And then she closed her eyes again, and waited for the final crash.

Hours later she was still very much as she had been when she started out that day, apart from the fact that one of her shoulders was badly bruised and she was dreadfully cold. Someone—she thought it was the navigator—had placed a coat about her shoulders, and she sat huddling it round her, while the freezing cold still successfully bit into every part part of her limbs, and it was more than she could do to prevent her teeth from chattering.

Near to her there were other people, striving to keep warm—the woman with the child had a broken arm, and she kept moaning in pain, and Rose had cradled the terrified infant in her own arms, until the air hostess had relieved her of it. But the air hostess had so many tasks to perform, and was being so extraordinarily plucky about the way in which she went about them, that Rose simply had to offer to take the child again, and as she sat there with the tiny body cuddled up close in her arms, and the enormous stars dipped and wheeled above her, she was at moments completely certain that this was only part of a nightmare.

If it hadn't been just a nightmare they really would have crashed, and everything would be over by now. The aircraft would have burst into flames, no one would have escaped, and when daylight dawned only their charred bodies would be found by the anxious searchers.

But, being just part of a nightmare, they had all escaped—serious injury, that is. There were a good many minor casualties, and the first officer had a couple of broken ribs. The pilot kept going round and endeavouring to put a little heart into each of them, the medal ribbons and the captain's indications of rank on his sleeve no longer showing, for the coat was acting as a pillow for the woman with the broken arm. Rose, when she looked at him through the star-pricked gloom and realized that he must be feeling the cold intensely, bereft, as he was, of his jacket, felt passionately thankful for his sake, as well as her own, that he had brought off a miracle, and that the only damage caused to his aircraft in landing was a smashed undercarriage.

He approached her now as she sat with the sleeping baby in her arms, and told her that dawn wasn't far off. And as soon as it was daylight help would reach them, and once help reached them there would be food and warm beds—and, perhaps what they wanted more than anything else, hot and reviving drinks!

Rose watched the first pink light come stealing over the snow peaks. It was like a blush, she thought, in a bemused fashion—like a blush on the face of a very young girl. And when it spread wildly in all directions, and the sun appeared like a ball of fire, the numbness which had every part of her in its grip seemed to melt a little, and it was almost as if a feeling of hope invaded her heart.

Later she was assisted down the mountain-side and into a car, and very soon after that she was in bed in the wooden-walled room of a little inn. She slept beneath the huge feather-filled quilt as if she had no intention ever of waking again; but when she finally did wake a rosy-cheeked daughter of the inkeeper brought her a bowl of wonderful broth which actually seemed to put new life into her, and although her shoulder was very sore and she had difficulty in dressing, once she finally was dressed she was able to insist that she didn't need any special attention. The mother with the baby had been taken straight to hospital, and one or two elderly passengers had also received priority treatment. But Rose had been sleeping so peacefully that no one had disturbed her, and when she made her way out into the sunshine she was glad that she was still up here in the mountains, and had not been whisked away to so-called civilization.

Here in the mountains, with all the gladness of a new day about her, flowery meadows like flowery skirts trailing down to the valley, and the shining peaks above her, she could almost blot out the intervening months and believe that she was still at Gerhardt and this was one of the trips up into the mountains they had sometimes made. In which case there would be a mistress ready to supervise everything, and she would have nothing at all to worry about, and life would be quite uncomplicated. The future would be just something that someone would take care of.

And it was when she thought of that that she realized she was no longer living in the past, and that it was the future that had caught up with her, and which from now on she had got to cope with alone. There was no one—*no one*—who would have any say in her affairs, and where she went from here, and when she went, was something that concerned only herself.

But she felt so unutterably weary, and so deathly tired still, and the gnawing pain in her shoulder made her feel a little sick. The thought that she had no one to turn to almost appalled her, for she was used to turning to someone, and this wasn't a very good time to start standing on one's own feet. Not when she dreaded even the thought of the future, when it seemed nothing but a barren wilderness stretching in front of her, when her heart was sick with longing for even the sound of one man's voice—just to hear him say: "Poor little Rose!" in a lightly compassionate tone, while he smiled at her as if she was somehow very young and foolish and ought not to entertain ideas about carving out a career for herself, and living in a flat in Paris.

She stared through eyes that were suddenly so full of tears that there wasn't any view at all of the village street, and although the sun felt hot as she sat on a bench outside the inn, her hands and her feet and every part of her was cold.

She was cold with dread—dread of her empty future.

A car drew up before the inn, but she hardly noticed it as the single passenger alighted and

173

said something to the driver, who drove off as if he had received instructions to turn, or perhaps to disappear altogether. Rose only partly realized that the car was moving off again, and then she felt someone standing beside her, and a hand touched her shoulder. A voice that was ragged with feeling spoke her name.

"Rose!"

She looked up. The tears were still there in her eyes, and it was impossible to blink them away in such a hurry that she could see clearly, and as it was, the familiar figure that she did vaguely make out through the blur could be nothing more than a figment of her slightly fevered imagination—or so she thought.

"Rose!" He sat down on the bench beside her and put both arms around her and held her as if she was a treasure he had recovered. "Oh, Rose!" he whispered.

And although a man wearing a battered hat and enormously thick-soled boots with spikes in them was marshalling a couple of cows with bells jangling on leather collars round their necks through the village, and a child was standing still and watching them with interest, he started to kiss away all the tears from her eyes.

CHAPTER XVII

ABOUT ten minutes later Rose became aware of the child, but by that time the cows had disappeared, and so had the man with the battered hat. Sir Laurence, after striving to extract information from her as to the extent of bruising her shoulder had suffered, and whether or not she was hurt anywhere else, stood up and pulled her gently to her feet, looking into her bemused eyes.

"Isn't there somewhere where we can be alone, Rose?" he asked. "I can't go on talking to you out here."

"There's a little sitting-room," she said. But she sounded like someone who was only half awake, and by no means certain that she was even half awake. "It wasn't occupied a little while ago."

"Then we'll go there," he said.

Inside the sitting-room, with its bowl of blue gentians on a centre table, he put her into the one comfortable chair and then stood looking down at her. The colour rolled hotly, painfully over her face and neck, and all her pallor vanished. Of course he hadn't really kissed her—that had been just part of an hallucination following upon the utter amazement of seeing him so suddenly—and if he had, well, it was because the sight of her had probably upset him. She knew she was looking shocked and strained, in spite of her excellent night's rest, and although she was wearing a fresh white blouse with her suit, the suit itself bore evidence of one very long night's vigil during which it had had to make contact with the rough earth.

"I'm sorry," she apologized, the words tumbling in painful embarrassment from her lips, "that I was being rather—rather silly—when you arrived just now! There was no reason why I should sit there crying in the open, because everyone has been so kind to me—"

"Rose!" He took the seat beside her and bent over her and took hold of both her hands. It might have been the dimness of the little room, but she thought he looked grey and rather gaunt, but whether from fatigue or anxiety she found it impossible to decide. "Have you any idea what a nightmare time I've lived through—waiting first for news and then not certain how I was going to find you . . ."

His eyes held an expression she had never seen in them before, and it set her weary pulses pounding sluggishly, while concern because he looked as he did tugged at every sensitive nerve in her make-up.

"I—I can't think how you knew . . ."

"Then you really imagined I would go away and not—not concern myself about you any more? Rose!" The reproach in his voice hurt her very acutely. "I had every intention of calling on both you and Mrs. Wilson-Plunkett before I finally left, but you tore away from the flat and left me so suddenly . . . Rose," hardly able to enunciate, *"why* did you do it?"

"Leave—Rome, you mean?" she asked faintly.

"With nothing but a note left behind, and practically no money . . . Mrs. Wilson-Plunkett told me you couldn't have very much!"

"I had enough," she whispered.

"Of course I would have followed you to Paris." His hands tightened convulsively on hers, and he drew them up until they rested against his chest. "I did fly to Paris that same night, and it was when I arrived there that I heard that the afternoon flight"—he swallowed—"the afternoon flight was hours overdue! Rose, can you imagine how I felt? Can you, for one single instant, imagine how I felt?"

Her fingers trembled in his. She was beginning to believe now not only that he had kissed her, but that his arms had actually held her out there in the front of the inn as if he had lived with the nightmare certainty that the opportunity was never going to be his, and the miracle of finding her practically unhurt made him decline ever to part with her again. She was certain now that it wasn't just fatigue in his face, and his eyes looked as if he couldn't possibly have endured much more.

"But the last time you saw me," she breathed huskily, "you told me you had lost faith in everyone. I was certain you particularly meant me!"

"Darling, I wanted to hurt you," he told her. "You seemed to have so little belief in me—you thought me so weak—and rather despicable! You were so eager to believe that I would take back Heather—even marry Lola Bardoli!—although I had already asked you to marry me! You even thought I was willing to marry you in order to protect myself from two women I was afraid of! It made me feel—pretty sick!"

"But—why did you ask me to marry you?"

"Why?" He looked down at her with eyes so dark with concentrated feeling that, for the first time for weeks, the almost tragic suggestion of wistfulness that had dwelt at the back of her own large eyes seemed to vanish like morning mist when the sun touches it, and for the first time a gleam of actual hopefulness took its place and lit them.

"It wasn't only because—because you wanted to—take care of me . . .?"

"I've wanted to take care of you, my darling child," he told her, his voice so deep and quiet that it seemed to reach out and enfold her in a warm, protecting clasp, "from the moment I first saw you, when you no longer had either a mother or a father to do that for you! All through the five

177

years I liked to feel I was responsible for you I had a particular desire to make you happy, and when you came home to Enderby for holidays I loved seeing you there. Before I met Heather and, for some reason, lost my head about her, I had a kind of half-formed plan at the back of my mind that when you finished with school you and I would travel about together and see something of the world . . . I had even thought out all the places we would visit, and the kind of things we would do in those places! Rome was one of them! . . ." He looked down at the hands he was holding crushed against his chest, and the tenderness round his mouth was like a living, breathing thing. "There was so much I was going to show you in Rome! . . ."

"You did show me—quite a lot," she reminded him.

"Not nearly as much as your Italian admirers!" And then his eyes were lifted to her appealingly. "I failed you, Rose, because I met Heather . . . But I swear to you that if it was love I ever felt for her it died on the afternoon she left me waiting for her in the church at Farnhurst! By evening of that same day I wouldn't have taken her back under any circumstances, and the next day, when we drove to Enderby, I was so filled with rage because I'd been so abominably used—rage and nothing else!—that I wasn't really a safe person to be with! I even wanted to hurt you, who'd never done me any harm in your life!"

"Then you do believe that I—never would have done you any harm?" she managed in a slightly cracked voice, because weariness was rushing up over her again, her bruised shoulder was aching like a toothache, and exhaustion showed plainly in her face.

"My beloved little Rose!" He went down on his knees beside her and gathered her close in his arms. "I ought not to be talking to you like this now—I'm taking you back in the car I hired to Zurich, where that shoulder of yours is going to be looked at, and a doctor will tell me whether you really are all right—but before we leave here you must understand how much I love you! Your eyes have haunted me ever since that last night at Enderby, and when I saw you again in Rome I knew that if only I'd had the sense and waited . . .!"

He groaned suddenly, so full of regret for the wasted weeks and months that she could almost feel it coursing through him, and her own love yearned to comfort and reassure him. She nestled against him like a tired child, and although her eyes were so heavy that she could hardly lift them to his face, she did manage to do so.

"It doesn't matter now," she whispered, "so long as you do know—now—that Heather wasn't so important . . ."

"She wasn't in the least important," he assured her, almost fiercely. "I only thought she was! But you—you, my adored, most precious, heart's-darling of a Rose!—so long as I live you'll be the only really important thing in my life! The one thing that will *make* my life worth living! . . . That is," he added, so humbly and pleadingly that it almost hurt her, "if you think you can trust me, Rose? To look after you and cherish you as a man cherishes a beloved wife! If you'll think again and then say 'yes' and marry me!"

For answer Rose again lifted her face to his, and this time her eyes openly implored him to kiss her. She wasn't capable just then of pretence—she hadn't any pride, or anything remotely resembling pride where he was concerned, and he had said enough to fill her with a rapture that would grow greater as her weariness ebbed. But just then she wanted to feel the touch of his lips, as she had felt it once before—not merely on her wet eyelids, but on her quivering lips . . . And he bent at once and touched those lips so tenderly

with his own, with such an instantaneous response
to the appeal in her eyes, that her arms lifted and
clung about his neck.

He whispered like a man who had lived through
too many kinds of emotion in the past few hours
to be capable of any sort of dissimulation either:

"Oh, Rose, Rose, Rose . . .!"

And then he kissed her mouth again, passion
that he was striving hard to suppress because he
felt it was so utterly unfair to her just then fight-
ing frantically to break through to the surface,
and fanning a feeble flame of passion in her that
gradually grew stronger . . .

On the way to Zurich he sat with her on the
back seat of the car, and held her in his arms so
that the twists and turns of the road didn't jar
her. At the hospital, where it was discovered that
nothing very serious was the matter with her
shoulder and that all she really needed was a
chance to rest and recover herself, with the assistance of a sedative to help overcome shock, she
was treated rather like a heroine who had survived an experience which might so easily have
proved fatal.

Amongst the other passengers there were no
serious casualties, and even the mother with the
baby was being permitted to fly home. Rose said
good-bye to her and to the baby, and then Sir Laurence took her to an hotel where he forced her to
eat a certain amount of lunch. She was looking a
little more like herself, but the sight of her worried him acutely, especially the heavy mauve shadows under her eyes, although the eyes themselves
smiled at him happily and reassuringly whenever
she caught him watching her. He was anxious to
get her back to Rome, but there was the question
of the journey, and he was afraid she might
shrink from the thought of flying.

But when he suggested to her that it would be
quicker and less trying for her if she could face

up to it, she answered at once that she could face up to anything with him. And she meant it. She slid her hand across the table to him, and he took it and squeezed it hard.

"And I'm not really afraid of air travel," she assured him. "But for this—this disaster, if you can call it that—we might never have found out how much we mean to each other!"

"All the same," he replied soberly, retaining her hand, "it's something I would far rather you had been spared!"

He put through a telephone call to Mrs. Wilson-Plunkett in Rome, and the widow all but burst into tears of relief with the receiver in her hand when she heard that Rose was not so very much the worse for her experience. She agreed that it was wise to keep her in Zurich for that night, and sent loving messages to Rose and the assurance that she was longing to see her again, and that the instant she arrived back at the hotel she would be put to bed and made a great fuss of.

The tears once more rolled down Rose's cheeks when Sir Laurence passed on these messages to her, and she knew that she had been absolutely right about Mrs. Wilson-Plunkett from the beginning. She was kindness and generosity itself, and apparently she bore Rose no ill-will for leaving her with so little consideration for the shock and anxiety her departure might cause her. On the contrary, Rose felt certain that she quite understood why she had left as she did, and would never reproach her for it. She might even have done the same thing under similar circumstances!

Rose went to bed that night with a dose of the sedative mixture that had been made up for her, and Sir Laurence sat beside her bed and held her hand until she fell asleep. It didn't strike her as at all strange and unorthodox that he should be sitting there, and she felt absolutely safe and contented knowing that he was near her. Just before

181

she fell asleep he bent over her and kissed her gently, her eyes, her brow and her lips, and then let his hand rest on the red flame of hair that was curling so brightly on the pillow.

And long after she was asleep and breathing tranquilly he still sat beside the bed, anxious least some sort of a nightmare resulting from her experiences might wake her, and she would be terrified to find herself alone.

The following morning, when they boarded the airliner for Rome, she could sense his anxiety for her in the way he held her hand during the take-off, and not even when their seat-belts were unfastened and the moment of tension was passed did he let go her hand. She could feel his fingers clasping hers, so vitally and so strongly, that they would have given her courage under any circumstances, and she looked round and up at him with a little smile of purest adoration in her eyes.

He caught his breath as he looked into those eyes, and although there was an air hostess in the aisle, carrying magazines and twists of barley-sugar to passengers, he slipped his arm behind her and drew her head to rest against his shoulder.

"Rose," he told her, his lips moving close to her ear, "I want us to be married almost immediately —within a few days! I shan't rest until you belong to me, and I can really look after you. So will a few days be long enough for you to get used to the idea of becoming my wife?"

"Of course," she answered, and repeated, "of course!" with her eyes still looking straight into his.

"I'm afraid there won't be any white wedding for you, my darling," he murmured regretfully, inhaling the scent of her hair and wishing more ardently that he had wished for anything in his life that they were alone, so that he could bury his lips in it. "For one thing, there won't be time

—and even if there was . . ." And then he broke off. "But if it's what you would really like, dearest—and you're so young and lovely that you oughtn't to be deprived of anything!—I will wait for you! Mrs. Wilson-Plunkett would fix things up—"

"No, no!" she breathed, and clutched convulsively at his hand. "It isn't what I like. I—at least, if I'd like it, I wouldn't let you go through *that* again! . . . Oh, Lance," looking at him reproachfully, "you don't imagine I'm as self-centred as all that?"

"No, Rose." He smiled at her tenderly. "But I'm not self-centred either, and I have no fears that you would keep me waiting!" Nevertheless, the almost convulsive pressure of his arm against her convinced her that he would never quite forget his experiences that sunny October day in far-away Farnhurst church. "But listen, darling" —his voice was suddenly urgent and entreating —"the thing I want is you, and although we may have to put up with a Civil Marriage we can always have a church service specially said for us afterwards when we get back to Enderby. You'd like that, wouldn't you?"

"Yes," she whispered, "I would!" Her eyes smiled at him because he understood so well. "And when will we go back to Enderby?" with sudden eagerness.

"Quite soon, if that's what you wish." He explained: "I cancelled, of course, my plans to go to America when — well, when you flew away from me so suddenly," with the first hint of real reproach in his eyes as well as his voice. "But there's no reason why we shouldn't have a honeymoon in the Bahamas. What would you like to do, Rose?"

She thought for a moment.

"What would you like to do?" she asked.

She felt his breath stirring her hair, and the air hostess seemed to be keeping very discreetly

183

out of their way—perhaps because she knew that
Rose had been one of the passengers in the aircraft that had crashed over the Alps—dazzling
white peaks they were flying over now—and she
understood the anxiety of the man beside her,
who was almost certainly someone very near and
dear to her indeed. His efforts to keep her completely diverted seemed to be working very well.

"I don't mind what we do, sweetheart," he told
her, "so long as we do it together! One place is as
good as another when all you want is one particular woman for your wife!" so low that the words
all but missed her.

But he knew they didn't, because her fingers
turned and clung to his.

"Lance—Lance," she said after a moment, during which she seemed to be thinking again, "had
you really intended to leave Rome so suddenly, or
was it because of—because of me?"

"The answer is that it was because of you,"
with a wry twist of his lips.

She looked up at him with a return of the sha-
dowed look.

"But you do understand that I came there to the
flat that day—that last day when you were packing!—because Signora Bardoli said . . ."

"What did Lola say?" one eyebrow ascending.

Rose flushed deliciously.

"She said—she seemed to think that—that _I_
could do something to prevent you going!" She
played agitatedly with his fingers. "You see,
Lance," her eyes very clear, and young, and hon-
est, "she knew that I—that I was in love with
you—and so, for that matter, did Heather . . . !"

The wry expression deepened round his mouth.

"Everyone, apparently, but me knew the one
thing I could never be certain about! Why was I
so blind?"

"I really can't think." She sounded so much
ashamed of herself. "I must have been terribly

184

transparent. Horribly transparent," looking upwards at him in confusion.

"But I had to wait to be certain until Mrs. Wilson-Plunkett told me on the day you left your farewell note!" His fingers imprisoned her wrist, feeling the shy pulse bounding. "Do you know what she said to me, Rose? She was so angry at what had happened to you, and my wilful blindness, as she called it, that she delivered me a lecture I'm hardly likely to forget! She pointed out to me the one thing that should have been clear to me from the beginning, and that was that you and I were born into this world specially for one another, and for absolutely no one else! She accused me of confusing the issues, as she put it, and all but driving you into the arms of another man—by whom I think she must have meant Prince Paul de Lippi! Or did she imagine you liked Camillo best?"

"She *knew* I wouldn't marry either of them," Rose answered.

"And you were never once tempted?" looking at the top of her head.

"Of course not," almost indignantly. "But I did actually like Camillo best—he's rather a dear, and in spite of the fact that I told him I hadn't any money he *did* ask me to marry him!" anxious to defend him from the accusation which Sir Laurence himself had once brought against him, and that was that he was out to marry an heiress.

"Good for Camillo!" Sir Laurence answered approvingly. "But then, of course, no man in his senses wouldn't want to marry you, Rose," he concluded, touching her soft cheek adoringly, and she refrained from making the obvious answer.

They looked at each other for a very long moment with all their hearts in their eyes, and then the man remarked appreciatively:

"So Lola Bardoli thought you could stop me from leaving Rome! She too, seems to have had a great deal of perception!"

"She said that it was the wrong time for you to leave Rome, and that you were engaged on work that would suffer if you went away so suddenly. And that's why it's occurred to me, Lance," with sudden adorable shyness, "that from your point of view a honeymoon is going to mean an interruption to that work, isn't it? Whereas if we didn't have the honeymoon—at least, not yet—and stayed on in Rome . . ."

"At the flat, you mean?"

"Yes." She could feel her heart pounding while she waited for him to express his own views, and when he did so there was tremendous tenderness in his eyes.

"Rose, my own darling, do you seriously mean that you would forego a honeymoon and go straight back to the flat with me after you had become Lady Laurence Melville? A bride content to watch a husband work?"

"Well," leaning against him so that he could feel the warmth of her slender body and craved once more to be alone with her, "you wouldn't be working all the time, and I loved the flat! And I do want you to finish what you began in Rome!"

The expression in his eyes was inexplicable, but once again she felt his breath stirring her hair.

"It would only take a few weeks," he admitted.

"And there's quite a lot we could still find to do in Rome. And before we returned to England we could have a week or so at some little coastal fishing village. That would give you a coating of tan, and set you up for the winter." He looked down at her thoughtfully. "And in the autumn we could return to Enderby!" He heard her catch her breath. "A year, Rose—a whole year out of your life, and you'll be twenty by the time you return—twenty and a wife! My wife!"

"And I love Enderby in the autumn," she whispered, not merely because it was true, but because his words had set her trembling inwardly—deep, deep down inside her—and for a few minutes she could hardly bear to meet his eyes.

The aeroplane was climbing steeply into a world of blue. The ice-cold peaks dropped away below them, and soon they were no longer flying over mountains at all, but travelling smoothly across a shimmer of blue sea in the direction of Rome.

Rose lay back, completely relaxed, against her seat and beside her Sir Laurence, relaxed also. She was no longer afraid, he knew—although there had been one or two moments of fear at the beginning of the flight—and she was completely happy. And so for that matter was he.

CHAPTER XVIII

MUCH later that day Mrs. Wilson-Plunkett lifted her glass in a toast.

"To you both!" she said. "To all the happiness you both deserve, although I think you, Sir Laurence deserve it a little less than Rose, for at least she always knew her own mind, whereas you were inclined to complicate matters!"

But Sir Laurence smiled at her with complete affability above the rim of his own glass, and in his heart he knew that he could do nothing less than agree with her.

Dinner had been served to them in Mrs. Wilson-Plunkett's own suite, for she had decided against permitting Rose the excitement and possible exhaustion of going down to the dining-room, and the pleasant little sitting-room that Rose had never expected to see again looked gay with flowers. The table sparkled with more flowers, silver and glass. Rose was wearing her little black cocktail dress, and it had a tiny upstanding collar that framed her face, and there was a single row of pearls about the slender white column of her throat. There was much less exhaustion in her face, and her eyes looked like green stars whenever they encountered Sir Laurence's direct gaze.

"Leave everything to me," Mrs. Wilson-Plunkett said when the waiter had departed after bringing in coffee and liqueurs. "*I'll* see to it that Rose is all ready for you by the end of the week, Sir Laurence. You must at least give her a week. And although I don't really approve of this idea of taking her straight to your flat—well, if that's what you both want to do I won't try and make you change your minds. But you needn't bother about fishing villages after that. My sister has a

Palazzo in Venice—one of those huge, rather mouldering places where you could, nevertheless, be extremely comfortable if I give instructions for a corner of it to be got ready for you. And there are maids left behind who will look after you. You'll be able to sun yourselves on the Lido, drift in the evenings in a gondola on one of the canals—and the gondolier will serenade you, Rose, because you're just the type to be serenaded by a gondolier!—and when you go back at night you'll have your balcony to sit on, and the moon, the palaces on the farther bank—all the romance of Venice!"

Rose smiled at her—loving her for her enthusiasm, for her eagerness to be of help to them, and also secretly more than thrilled by the picture she painted. Sir Laurence looked at Rose and saw that the girl's eyes were wide and becoming a trifle bemused. He thought she had had about enough for one day.

"Just as you say, Mrs. Wilson-Plunkett," he agreed. "If Rose would like Venice, then I haven't any objections at all, and so long as your mouldering palace doesn't fall down on us I'm sure we'll be delightfully happy—and very much in your debt!" Then he reached out a hand to Rose. "But you're tired, my darling—I really do think you ought to go to bed, you know!"

Mrs. Wilson-Plunkett was nothing if not tactful. She drained the remains of some champagne in her glass, decided that she didn't want any coffee, and stood up.

"I promised Lady Bailey I'd play bridge with her tonight," she announced, "and I'm already rather late. Once Sir Laurence has left, Rose, I'll pop up and make sure that you're comfortably settled in bed, and the chambermaid will be coming in to help you if you want any help with your undressing." She beamed at them both, and then looked directly at Sir Laurence. "No protracted good nights, but you can come in and see her as early as you like in the morning. We'll even welcome you for breakfast!"

Once she had left the room, her black velvet and her diamonds bustling away along the corridor, Sir Laurence stood up and went round the table until he stood behind Rose's chair. He put his hands on her shoulders and drew her out of the chair, turning her round to face him as soon as she was on her feet.

"Rose!" he whispered. "My Rose! . . ."

He drew her into his arms and held her closely, and yet more closely. She knew now that he really was striving to keep passion in check, but her own longing for him was greater than anything she had ever felt in her life before. She wound her slim arms upwards about his neck and held him tightly, dreading the moment when she had to let him go. Once more her lips pleaded for his kisses.

He gave them to her, long, hungry kisses that claimed her, and set every sensitive nerve in her body responding wildly. When at last he let her go they were both a little pale, and he was full of remorse.

"Mrs. Wilson-Plunkett wouldn't approve of this at all, Rose!" he told her. "She said 'no protracted good nights'—And I ought to have more sense! But I love you so much! . . . Oh, darling, I love you so much!"

"And I," Rose told him truthfully, "have loved you ever since I was fourteen. Not in the way I love you now, but . . ." She sighed as she leaned against him. "It's been a long time loving you, and when you decided to marry Heather I nearly broke my heart! The night before the wedding ceremony was to have taken place I think it actually did crack a little bit, because I almost died of misery!"

"Oh, Rose!" he breathed, and held her passionately close again.

She drew herself gently away from him. Then she remembered something.

"Do you know, Lance," she said, "I threw a coin into the fountain—the Fontana de Trevi—and it brought me back to Rome!" Her eyes were shining suddenly. "I also made a wish. Shall I tell you what that wish was! Part of it came true when I suddenly saw you again in Rome, and the other part—"

"Yes?" he whispered tenderly, taking her back into his arms while she made her confession. "What was the other part of your wish, sweetheart?"

"Can't you possibly guess?" she inquired, looking up at him.

"I'd rather you told me."

"Then", she smiled into his eyes, gently stroked his face—"it was that you would find happiness again, Lance, my beloved! I couldn't bear it when I knew you were unhappy!"

"And if I'd found happiness with someone else?" he asked very slowly.

"Then I wouldn't really have minded—at least I would, of course, have minded terribly, but—more than anything else I wanted you to be happy!"

And all he could say then, as he buried his face in her hair, was, rather helplessly:

"Oh, Rose!"

THE END

FREE Harlequin romance catalogue

A complete listing of all the titles currently available.

Harlequin Reader Service

IN THE U.S.A.
1440 South Priest Dr., Tempe, AZ 85281

IN CANADA
649 Ontario St., Stratford, Ontario N5A 6W2

Please send me my FREE Harlequin Reader Service Catalogue.

Name _____

Address _____

City _____

State/Prov. _____ Zip/Postal _____